THE
TIME
SEER

ALSO BY RICHARD PHILLIPS

The Endarian Prophecy

The Rho Agenda

The Rho Agenda Inception

The Rho Agenda Assimilation

THE
TIME
SEER

THE ENDARIAN PROPHECY
RICHARD PHILLIPS

Text copyright © 2020 by Richard Phillips
All rights reserved.

Published by 47North, Seattle

www.apub.com

Amazon, the Amazon logo, and 47North are trademarks of Amazon.com, Inc., or its affiliates.

ISBN-13: 9781542015097
ISBN-10: 154201509X

Cover design by Shasti O'Leary Soudant

Printed in the United States of America

THE
TIME
SEER

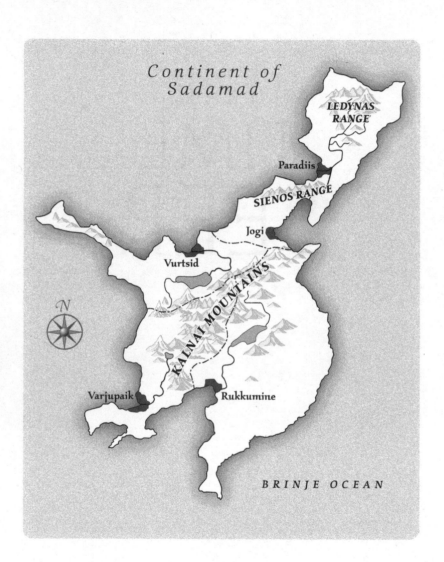

PART I

Long have I labored to perfect my time-sight to find the
one for whom I have searched all the futures branching
before me. Never did I suspect that his unbridled ability
might be beyond my power to control.

—From the *Scroll of Landrel*

1

Carol stepped out of the longboat and climbed the ladder onto the pier as twilight claimed the evening. As she gazed at the detritus mounded along the lengthy pier, she paused.

"This doesn't feel right."

Arn stepped up beside her. "That's because it isn't."

Carol watched Princess Kimber and Prince Galad scale the rungs and climb up onto the dock. Although Kim stood six feet tall, her fully Endarian brother towered over her, his straight black hair swirling around his shoulders in the chill breeze. But it was the look of horror on Kim's face that sent a chill through Carol's body.

The place reeked with the lingering remnants of foul magic of a sort that Carol had never encountered. She couldn't shake a vague, haunting feeling. Was this the spot from which Kragan had summoned the swarm of sea dragons that attacked their two ships?

As Alan and his soldiers climbed onto the pier from the three other longboats, Carol's gaze was drawn to the piles of bones that covered the docks. She bent to the nearest corpse. The desiccated form looked ancient, but the clothes draped over the bones were fresh. The sight raised the fine hairs on the back of her neck.

"What in the name of the dark gods?" Arn asked as he examined the remains.

Carol moved from mound to mound. There were hundreds of bodies, all similar in that the clothing looked to be in crisp condition while the carcasses wrapped within appeared to have withered for years. The tallest of these people would have measured barely four feet. She knelt beside one adult skeleton and two tiny ones gathered into the woman's arms, their fingers intertwined. The images that the scene pulled into her mind spread a tightness from her throat into her chest.

A ragged gasp swung Carol's gaze to Kim. The bewilderment on her half sister's face mirrored the ache in Carol's soul.

"Kragan's work," Arn said, his right hand gripping Slaken's haft so tightly that the sinews stood out on his forearm.

"I've never seen this form of necrotic magic," Kim said. "It is an abomination. Nobody can channel that much life energy and survive. Not even Kragan."

A new dread built within Carol. Her eyes met Arn's, and she knew that he had come to the same conclusion.

"Unless," she said, "he's already retrieved a fragment of Landrel's Trident."

—◊◊◊—

It was after midnight when Arn and the rest of the company assembled around a wide and deep trench. Alan and his Forsworn had dug the massive hole using shovels they'd retrieved from various locations in the dead village of small buildings. Carol stood at the edge of the dark pit, peering into its depths, then turned around to face the bay. She reached into the ethereal planes and summoned an air elemental, Betep, using the being to lift her thirty feet into the air and solidify an invisible ledge for her to stand upon. Shifting her focus, she called forth Golich from the plane of fire, using the minor being to create dozens of light globes that illuminated the piers atop which the remains of hundreds of villagers lay scattered.

Only a day ago, these had been fishermen, their wives, and children, who gave this isolated village its life. Now, lit by the soft light of arcane orbs, her view of the colorful clothing that draped the piles of bones brought dampness to her eyes and tightened her throat. As if her mood had beckoned the cold, a frosty gust from the bay whipped stinging droplets into her face such that she couldn't tell whether water or tears leaked down her cheeks.

Carol gave the air elemental a series of new tasks, gently gathering the piles of remains and carrying them on the wind to settle into the pit. The groupings of bones and clothes painted pictures in her mind of frightened families tightly huddled together while Kragan funneled their life energy to raise the foul sea creatures. She hoped these people had died quickly, without pain. But her familiarity with Kragan and his methods made her doubt that.

Though she did her best to keep the bones and garments in the groupings within which they had been found, she soon realized that Betep was incapable of that degree of precision. In the end the mass grave became one contiguous jumble. With the piers swept clean, Carol settled to the ground and turned to face the trench.

Except for the sound of slow rain, silence ruled the night. No one spoke words of comfort. They had none to give. Beside Arn, Carol stretched out her right hand, wielding Kevir to send the mounds of earth flowing in to cover the bones.

When she turned her back on the mass grave, Arn placed his hand on her arm.

"You all right?"

"I'm empty," she said.

"Let's get out of this rain. You need to sleep."

"Not sure I can."

"Then you can rest in my arms."

"Only if you set your knife aside. Tonight, I need to feel your mind as well as your body."

Carol summoned a globe of soft light that allowed him to meet her gaze. The longing that he saw there stilled the words that almost made their way from his lips. Instead he took her by the hand and led her back toward the tiny house where they would spread their bedrolls on the floor.

He glanced at their she-vorg prisoner, Charna. She sat in the mud, legs and arms wrapped around the tree where he'd chained her. The jutting jaws that marked her breed opened, revealing her long canines. But it was the hatred in her eyes that stoked his satisfaction.

Arn opened the short door and ducked inside with Carol right behind him, her magic orb lighting the room where they would sleep. He shoved the table and chairs against the far wall to make room to spread their blankets on the wood floor. In doing so he blocked the door that led into a bedroom too small to comfortably accommodate them.

Disrobing, they hung their wet clothes over the chairs. Arn placed the sheath that held Slaken within reach of their bedding, and together they curled into their blankets. When Carol nestled into his enfolding arms, she settled her head on his chest and let sleep take her.

As tired as he was, Arn remained awake, savoring the feel of his wife's warm body against his. But it wasn't the pleasure of her touch that kept his eyes open for the better part of an hour. His dread of the dreams that haunted him did that.

But even such dread had its nemesis. Exhaustion.

2

Landrel clasped the mummified center finger loosely in his left palm, embracing its amplification of his time-sight. He commonly strode the winding paths of the futures that spun out before him, but Landrel still felt trepidation over the pull of this last fragment of the trident of magic amplification that he had created and then dismantled.

His family was his priority. More important than the Endarian people he'd once loved. More important than his magic. More important than his life. To save his eldest son, Landrel had wielded the forbidden necrotic life magic and, in so doing, sacrificed his position as king of Endar and undertaken a life of banishment.

The scene formed in Landrel's mind as brilliantly as he'd experienced it on that distant day.

Ten-year-old Dailus was never late to the family's evening dinner, a sacred time when Landrel extracted himself from his royal duties to sup with his wife and children and to discuss their day's doings. But on this night Dailus missed the entire meal.

Filled with worry, Landrel searched for his son. Despite having been told to restrict his play to the narrow beach on the south side of the lake, Dailus had strayed into the forest. Landrel found him lying beneath a blue spruce, his breathing so weak that at first Landrel believed him dead. The boy's left forearm was swollen, with veins of purple crawling up to his shoulder from twin punctures near his wrist. The sight sent a shudder through Landrel. The bite of a tree adder.

Landrel tried absorbing the wound into himself, but the poison had been in the boy's body for too long. He was on the verge of death. And then, in Landrel's arms, Dailus stepped across that boundary.

As if it felt his misery, the lonely howl of a wolf pulled Landrel's gaze from his son's face to that of the animal that stood at the edge of the clearing, surrounded by a half dozen yelping pups. Knowing that what he was about to do was sacrilege, Landrel did it anyway. If a person had been nearby instead of wolves, the life energies would have easily matched. Instead he needed to funnel all seven of these lives into his son.

The tendrils of his magic reached into the wolf and her pups, turning their howls and yaps into shrieks. The wielder transferred their essence into Dailus's freshly dead body, heedless of the risk that this use of necrotic life magic might infuse wolfish traits into his son, perhaps even altering Dailus's progeny.

That action forever changed Landrel's life and the lives of his family. Although no wolflike traits manifested within Dailus, the same could not be said of his children and grandchildren. When the Endarian High Council discovered the wolf-human hybrid infants, they deposed Landrel and ordered the execution of Dailus and his children.

Landrel instead used the mystic trident to defend his family. His fury tempted him to pull down the royal palace and the walled city it guarded. Yet, showing mercy, he slew only those who tried to stop him from escaping with his clan, disappearing onto the windswept Northeastern Plains.

Landrel straightened, extracting himself from his memory. Within the present day, he sensed death's approach. He had long foreseen the enemy who was coming for him, and he could see no future wherein both he and his children survived.

But Landrel found one future to which he'd dedicated the last six years of his mortal existence, arranging the clockwork pieces to bring it about.

He wove his way through the futures that spilled out before him, his need pulling him toward the man he would reach through time to pass his artifact to. A distant vision appeared through the mists of time, attaining crystal clarity as his essence flowed forward. Inside a small cottage slept the man toward whom Landrel's vision pulled him. A pale beam of moonlight broke through the rain clouds and speared through the window to illuminate the human's face. His features had been sharpened by years of killing, one ear sliced to a point that poked through his curly brown locks.

Had Landrel entered this room in person, his target would have sensed a presence and grabbed the black knife from the spot where it rested on the floor beside his bedding. But only Landrel's mind made this journey through time.

Ignoring the familiar woman who slept beside the assassin, Landrel shifted his gaze to the knife's haft. The runes on the handle twisted the moonlight until it seemed to crawl across their surface, the sight so intriguing that it almost broke Landrel's concentration. But this was the moment to reveal the arcane gift hidden within the man's prized weapon.

Landrel placed an ethereal hand on the human's forehead and then made the connection that linked his time-sight to the untrained talent the assassin possessed. A silent whisper escaped Landrel's lips as the man stirred in his sleep.

"Time to embrace your destiny."

—◇◇◇—

Arn stepped out onto the plain, where golden knee-high grass waved in the stiff morning breeze. The rustle of its seed-laden stems was the only sound to make its way to his ears. Smoke tickled his nostrils, and he turned, looking for the source. The lonely two-story house on the vast expanse was familiar. Arn had been here before, in another dream, not so long ago. He reluctantly walked toward the front door, knowing who awaited him inside.

He placed his hand on the door handle, hesitated, then opened it and entered. The figure hunched over the table didn't look up. Wind, having made its way into the room in Arn's company, swirled the Endarian's midnight-colored hair.

Arn closed the portal and approached Landrel from behind, an uneasy premonition nibbling at the corner of his mind. But rather than scrawling on parchment, as Arn had found him doing on a previous occasion, the wielder of the nine magics focused his gaze upon a rectangular wooden basin, over a foot long and a handbreadth wide and deep. When Arn stepped to Landrel's side, he saw what held the ancient wielder's attention.

At the bottom of the container lay Slaken.

When Arn reached for the knife, Landrel grabbed Arn's wrist, and Arn found himself frozen, unable to resist as the wielder pulled his hand forward. When his hand was directly above the basin, the tip of the blade rose to meet it, cutting deeply into his palm, then slicing upward toward his wrist. Although Arn felt no pain, blood poured from the wound, flowing down the blade and onto the runed haft.

The glyphs pulsed with the rhythm of Arn's heart, soaking in his blood as if trying to quench a vast thirst. Cold crept up his arm, spreading from his right shoulder and into his chest and neck. Arn found his vision dimming, the magical handle of his knife seeming to become indistinct, as if turning to smoke.

And as the mystic knife dissolved before his eyes, Arn's throat clenched, blocking the scream building within.

—◊—

Arn awoke with a start, sitting bolt upright on the floor, startling Carol awake beside him.

She reached out to place a hand on his arm.

"What's wrong?" she asked, summoning a glowing orb to light the small room.

Arn reached out and placed his hand on Slaken's haft, relieved to find the weapon resting safely in its leather sheath.

"Arn?"

He exhaled, surprised that he had been holding his breath, then rubbed his face with both hands as he strove to clear the dream's remnants from his head.

"It's okay, love. Just a nightmare. You can go back to sleep."

Arn kissed her, then threw off his blanket and began dressing. He had no idea of the time, just that it was still dark out. He desired no more sleep.

"Was it another dream of Landrel?"

"Yes."

"More revelations about his prophecy?"

"He showed me how to destroy Slaken."

"Do you believe he wants that?"

Ducking to avoid a rafter, Arn stepped past the short table to stare out the window into the damp night, his thoughts centered on the dream. Years ago, he'd performed a different blood ritual to create his bond with the magical blade and the four elementals trapped within its haft. No other could pick up the knife without being consumed.

"Yes."

"Because it blocks your time-sight whenever you wear or hold it."

11

Her words carried the certainty of conviction. She believed, as Arn did, that the long-dead magic wielder had somehow reached through the ages to urge Arn to fully develop his own rare talent. But Slaken damped Arn's sense of the possible futures that roiled around him, leaving Arn with only preternatural intuition.

His wife stepped up behind him, gently wrapping her arms around Arn and pulling him close. Her warm breath brushed his right ear.

"You don't have to destroy Slaken," she said. "Merely put it away while I help you explore your latent time magic."

"Slaken protects me from Kragan's mind magic. When the opportunity presents itself, the knife will enable me to get close enough to kill him."

Once again, a resumption of the argument that had driven a wedge between them before. Carol released him and stepped back.

When he turned to face her, she stood with her arms crossed over her long nightshirt.

"Do you remember how we fought alongside each other after you dropped Slaken aboard the *Saimniece*, our minds linked as you wielded your time-sight? All I'm asking is that you place more faith in us than in that dark-spawned knife."

Arn's response felt wrong as it left his lips.

"Wielded my time-sight? I was completely lost in it. Had you not been there, the horse-headed sea creatures would have killed me like wolves on a fawn."

Carol uncrossed her arms and stepped close, her lips pressed into a tight line.

"But I was there. And it was what I saw in your visions that enabled me to wield my magic in the only way that could have saved our companions and ourselves. Can't you see what a team we can become if you let me help you?"

Arn paused to look into Carol's imploring eyes, striving to master his conflicting emotions. His love for this woman was nearly all-consuming but couldn't quench his thirst for vengeance against Charna and Kragan.

The only thing that prevented him from walking out into the rain to where Charna was chained to a tree and slitting her throat was his need for her to guide him to her master. Then he would wield Slaken for the last time. Only then could he set the knife aside.

"I'm sorry," Arn said.

He opened the door and ducked through it into the night's driving rain, feeling the water pelt his face and run down his neck. Still his black Endarian shirt and trousers repelled the moisture, leaving the skin they covered warm and dry.

He stalked past the tree where he had chained Charna's arms. He saw her by the light shining from the window in the cottage he'd just left. The warrior sat hugging the tree in a puddle. Rain sluiced off the muzzle that jutted two inches from her otherwise human-looking face as she twisted her head to look back at him. The dim illumination failed to hide the hatred that shone in her eyes. Arn's right hand moved to Slaken as if in response to its summons. He abruptly turned and walked away.

Someday soon he would answer Slaken's call. But not tonight.

—⁂—

Carol watched Arn walk out into the storm and shut the door behind him without a glance back. If she wanted, she could have summoned an air elemental to stop the rain, but her frustration wouldn't allow her to reward her husband with comfort.

Her thoughts shifted to yesterday's battle with the sea dragons. So many of her companions had met the most gruesome of deaths, pulled into rending maws by the creatures' tentacle-like tails. If a sea monster hadn't knocked Slaken from Arn's hand, Carol couldn't have linked her mind with his. That link had let her experience the futures he saw and use her magic to influence which would come to pass. Even so, they had barely survived.

She knew the anger that propelled Arn toward the moment when he would kill the wielder he hunted. Arn had sought revenge ever since that evening when his five-year-old self watched from a hiding place as Kragan and Charna murdered his parents.

Landrel was somehow communicating with Arn through his dreams. Carol was convinced that the long-dead wielder was attempting to show them that they could defeat Kragan, but only if Arn embraced his time-sight talent. But she feared that by pushing the man she loved to put aside his magical blade, she was also pushing him away.

Arn was the feared assassin people had named Blade. A killer, driven to use his talents to destroy Kragan. Was she selfish to ask her husband to suppress his warrior nature so she could use his foresight against the wielder? In the struggle for Endar Pass, Kragan's foul horde had killed her father too. She deserved vengeance as much as Arn did.

Carol turned to sit cross-legged on the floor beside the pack containing Landrel's Scroll. Removing it, she manipulated the twin rollers to unveil a section of the document she had read at least a dozen times since Arn's first dream meeting with the writer. Raising the brightness of her summoned light globe, she bent her head to study the words one more time. Surely by doing so she could find confirmation that she was doing the right thing.

As she read, she failed to notice how she slowly rocked herself back and forth.

—⁊⁊⁊—

On this rain-soaked night, Captain Joresh, in command of Kragan's company of resurrected heroes, followed the diminutive wielder to the top of a rocky outcropping. With his men guarding the lone approach to this elevated perch, he didn't worry that someone could threaten this master who had granted them a second chance at life. Why Kragan had ordered the halt and commanded Joresh to accompany him to this spot remained a mystery.

Although the downpour drenched the surrounding countryside, no droplets touched the ground for dozens of paces around Kragan. The wielder sat cross-legged on the stone ledge, illuminated by light that cast no shadows.

All sound suddenly stilled, leaving an unnatural silence that sent a shiver up Joresh's spine. The thought that perhaps Kragan intended to sacrifice him as part of the necrotic ritual he was initiating crossed the captain's mind. Joresh angrily dismissed the worry. If Kragan wanted to kill him, there was nothing Joresh could do to stop him. He was every bit as mortal as he had been in his previous life.

But when Kragan had summoned him and his companions from the land of the dead, the resurrected had all found themselves bound to Kragan's will. In all things that didn't conflict with his master's wishes, Joresh and the others could do as they pleased. Right now, he would continue to stand watch for as long as the wielder wanted.

—⁂—

Kragan felt his bond to Charna strengthen as he concentrated on their connection. The she-vorg was cold and wet, her arms chained around a tree, its rough bark just another discomfort among many. Rather than communicating with her tonight, Kragan had other intentions. Through the she-vorg's ears, Kragan heard a door open and then close, a sound that drew Charna's gaze. Silhouetted against the unnatural light shining out through the cottage window, Blade's dark form strode into the night.

The assassin approached Charna, then stopped to look down at her. Kragan was assailed by a strong desire to cast a spell through Charna's eyes and smite this wretched man who relentlessly hunted him. But the sight of the shadowy weapon sheathed at his side dissuaded the wielder. The presence of the warded knife made such a thing impossible.

Then Blade turned and stalked off into the dark.

Kragan shifted his concentration to the mystic link that allowed Charna to know his location. He couldn't just terminate the channel. Blade and the witch, Carol Rafel, would sense that Charna was lying if she attempted to direct their steps toward Kragan. Instead of breaking the connection, Kragan shifted Charna's magical link to a body he'd recently occupied, that of Queen Lielisks, now entombed within her city-state of Varjupaik. Just enough of Kragan's necrotic aura lingered within the corpse to make such redirection possible.

The effort took much longer than he'd imagined. Although Lielisks had been entombed for the weeks it took Kragan to travel from Varjupaik to his birthplace in the Zvejys village of Klampyne, he could still sense her corpse. Only the amplifying effects of his necklace enabled Kragan to wield necrotic life magic across such a distance.

Mystic energy flooded through Kragan, and he exulted in the power. He could only imagine the glory that would be his when he acquired all nine fragments from Landrel's shattered trident.

An image of the reconstructed weapon of mummified fingers formed with such clarity that he reached out to grasp it. But when his fingers closed around the trident that would make him a god, it dissolved into smoke.

Kragan redirected his attention to the task at hand. He did not allow Joresh to cry out as he funneled the captain's life essence through the channel. Increasing the power of his sending, Kragan pulled the queen from the land of the dead to reanimate her corpse. Had he been much closer, he could have completely restored her life instead of granting her these minutes of torment, agony that Joresh would be forced to share.

When Kragan was satisfied that he had caused Charna's arcane sense of his location to orient toward the dead queen, he allowed death to claim both of his latest victims. Releasing his hold on Charna's mind, Kragan opened his eyes. Joresh lay faceup beside him, his bulging eyes staring sightlessly into the night sky.

As Kragan stared down at his former captain's dead body, a sigh escaped his lips at the thought of the objective that made this sacrifice necessary. He fingered the magical artifacts that hung from his neck. Even though he now possessed two of the nine magical fingers that Landrel had crafted into his trident of magic amplification, four others lay ensconced in time stones within the temples of the city-states of Rukkumine, Jogi, Vurtsid, and Paradiis.

Kragan needed to beat the Rafel witch to those artifacts. An image of the six mummified fingers hanging from his necklace blossomed in Kragan's mind, bringing a smile to his lips. With that collection of artifacts in his possession, he would be too powerful for even Carol Rafel to stand in his way. At that point, he could turn his attention back to the Endarian Continent and the retrieval of the final three fingers that Landrel had hidden there.

Kragan reached over and gently closed Joresh's eyelids. Rolling onto his knees, he leaned down to kiss the warrior's forehead and whisper a last farewell.

"Thank you, Captain. You have served me well."

3

Carol roused herself from her study of the scroll, stretching her stiff
muscles, as the first pale light of dawn filtered through the window. She
reached for Arn only to find that he had never returned to their bedding
on the wood floor of the tiny house. The memory of last night's argument pained her almost as much as the ache in her stiff neck.

She heard her brother, Alan, yelling orders, and the tromp of
booted feet told her that she was getting a late start to her day. Again she
wondered why Arn hadn't roused her. Nor had he stowed his bedroll.
To spend the night brooding was so unlike her husband.

She dressed in the Endarian traveling clothes that Queen Elan
had provided. Carol had kept them stowed dryly during the seagoing
portion of their journey to Sadamad. Unlike Arn's black uniform, her
clothes shifted colors to match their surroundings, just like those worn
by Galad and his few remaining mist warriors.

Carol packed her bedroll, hesitated, and then did the same for
Arn's. She slung her bundle over her shoulder but summoned Betep to

levitate the other. When she opened the door, she found Arn standing just outside. He turned toward her and smiled, showing no semblance of last night's anger.

"Why didn't you come back to bed?" she asked.

"Couldn't sleep. Wanted to let you get some rest."

When he leaned in to kiss her, she welcomed it, wrapping her arms around his neck. Relief lifted the weight of depression from her chest.

Arn righted himself, then reached around her to grab his bag as Carol released her magical hold. When they turned toward the company assembled in the street near Alan, Galad, and Kim, Carol noticed that the rain had given way to a soft drizzle, barely more than a fine mist.

Her eyes shifted to the *Milakais*, anchored a few dozen paces from the docks, where scores of fishing boats bobbed in the gentle swells. Several sailors worked to repair sails and rigging damaged in the battle against the creatures that Kragan had sent forth. Had it really been only yesterday?

She surveyed the docks and then shifted her gaze to the empty shops and houses. Alan's warriors had discovered fresh food in the larders and meals left half-eaten on tables. The small people who had previously occupied the town were simply gone. This morning's gloom amplified the eerie sensations she felt.

She walked up to the group of leaders who stood in conference with Alan. He turned to meet her, moisture gleaming on his shaved head and thickly muscled neck. But it was the smile on his face that disconcerted Carol. Over the weeks at sea, the near-constant banter of Alan's close companions, Bill Harrison and Quincy Long, had restored her brother's free-spirited nature, which the deaths of the men and women who served him had almost destroyed. But it was Katrin, her shaved pate exaggerating the exotic allure of the female warrior's face, who fanned the spark in Alan's eyes.

"So, Sister," Alan asked, "what are your orders?"

Carol turned to the assembled group of leaders. "Any recommendations?"

"We should immediately begin the pursuit," Alan said, "lest Kragan get too far ahead of us."

Prince Galad nodded in agreement. "By traveling within the time-mists I wield, we should be able to quickly catch the wielder and his party."

"High Lorness," interjected Quincy, gripping and releasing the hilt of his sheathed longsword. "With our reduced numbers and not knowing how many soldiers Kragan has with him, we may not be prepared for the encounter. If you're considering stripping the *Milakais* of its sailors, I don't think Tekelas will go along with the plan."

Carol pictured the female sea captain with the scar that disappeared behind her eyepatch and agreed.

Only thirty-nine of Alan's Forsworn had survived yesterday's sea battle. Counting Alan, Kim, Galad, Arn, and Carol, her company totaled only twoscore plus four. And they were saddled with the prisoner, Charna, who would guide them to Kragan.

As much as Carol was tempted to have Galad order the Endarian captain to relinquish some of her seventeen sailors, she wouldn't do so. The towering captain of the *Milakais* had done her duty in bringing them to this shore. Besides, such a small augmentation to Carol's company would make little difference in the outcome of the coming conflict. Alan and his Forsworn, supported by the combined magics of Carol, the sibling Endarians, and Arn, would have to be enough.

Carol looked into Arn's brown eyes and received all the encouragement she needed to make her decision.

"Have all provisions for our expedition been moved ashore?" she asked.

"We're prepared to march," Alan said, a note of anticipation in his voice.

"Send word to Captain Tekelas that I release her and her ship from duty. She is free to set sail for any other port of call she chooses."

With a nod to Quincy, Alan sent the lanky swordsman striding toward the boat that would carry him and his message out to the *Milakais*.

Carol shifted her eyes, locking them with those of her husband.

"It's time for Charna to remind us why we keep her alive."

—◊—

Charna watched as Blade walked to the tree to which he'd bound her, felt him unshackle her and roughly pull her to her feet. Having lost much of the circulation in her extremities during the chill, damp night, she almost stumbled and fell, but with supreme effort she righted herself. The she-vorg who had commanded Kragan's army during the battle for Endar Pass would never allow herself to show this human such weakness.

Blade cuffed her hands behind her back, then shoved her forward, toward the head of the column of bald warriors that Alan Rafel led out of the village and into the swamp that surrounded it, with the Rafel witch and the Endarian prince at his sides. And as the wielder strode forward, the muck solidified beneath her feet to form a firm path, two paces wide. Kim, the Endarian princess who had briefly been Charna's slave, followed Alan.

Charna sensed the impatience in the assassin who walked beside her, counting on her to guide them to Kragan. The direction in which she sensed the immortal wielder of dark magic had shifted to the northwest during the night. In truth, Charna wanted to bring these fools who believed themselves capable of killing her master into his presence. She couldn't wait to see the humans and Endarians writhing in their death throes as Kragan sucked life from their bodies.

The imagery that formed in her mind tugged her lips from a scowl into a smile. She risked a sideways glance at Blade. The assassin in black had stolen the enslaved princess from Charna in the border town of

Rork. Several times, this man had come closer to killing Charna than anyone else ever had. When Blade captured her at the height of the battle for the Endarian citadel, only her offer to lead him to Kragan had saved her.

She shifted her gaze back toward the Rafel witch, who was Blade's wife. Charna would relish the moment when Kragan killed this woman in front of Blade's eyes. She hoped that her master would allow her to tear open the assassin's throat with the same jutting jaws and two-inch canines that had ripped apart his mother and father. Even after a quarter of a century, she could still taste their rich blood as it poured into her mouth.

Ending Blade would form an even sweeter memory, one Charna would savor through all the years of her life.

4

Kalnai Foothills, West of Rukkumine
YOR 415, Mid-Summer

Kim walked into the rychly time-mist that Galad wielded, feeling as if she were struggling clear of a clutching bog. The zone where time moved at an accelerated pace cleared as a lighter-shaded fog shrouded the normal world she left behind. During the weeks they had sailed the sea, she'd almost forgotten what it was like to enter the time-magic her brother could channel. The disorientation that came with travers-ing the fogs caused many to lose all sense of direction. Galad's rare talent enabled him to wield two of the three branches of time magic simultaneously. In addition to summoning the slowing pomaly fogs and the accelerating rychly mists, he sensed what lay across the boundaries beyond which time moved at a different pace.

She savored the varying warmth of the sun. Instead of the brilliant orange disk that rode the daylight sky in the world of normal time, here it was a lighter smudge in a murky sky. Looking at the blighted sun made her dizzy, so she redirected her gaze at the trail the she-vorg prisoner set for them.

Alan's fanatical followers, the Forsworn, marched northwest across the surface of the swamp that would have surely claimed victims if not for Carol's magic. She had summoned an elemental to harden the muck and create a path through the bog. Two paces in front of Kim, Alan led the way, followed by Galad and Carol. Arn and his prisoner, Charna, walked a few paces to Kim's right. Bill Harrison, Quincy Long, and Katrin led the rest of the Forsworn along the path.

As Alan moved, Kim studied him. At just over six feet, Alan was Kim's equal in height, though his thickly muscled frame more than doubled her weight. The ax slung across his back had belonged to Ty, the Kanjari horseman who, alongside Arn and John, had rescued her from vorg slavers. Of these three men who had escorted her on the long trek from Rork to Kim's home in Endar Pass, only Arn remained alive.

A vivid memory blossomed in her mind as the real world faded.

—◊◊◊—

Kim stood on the stage inside the slaver's tavern, her hands bound so tightly in front of her that the rough cords cut into her wrists, breaking open scabs that were only beginning to form. Buried in intense distress, Kim tried to retreat within herself but was unable to escape the awfulness of her situation. Bandits and vorgs called out bids, their voices hoarse with anticipation of purchasing an Endarian princess.

Kim tried not to think of what they would do to her, but the abysmal thoughts consumed her.

With the rattle of chain mail, a burly she-vorg rose to her feet.

"One hundred gold."

A low moan of disappointment passed through the crowd, but nobody matched the she-vorg's offer.

A bell rang and the fat auctioneer's voice echoed through the hall. "Sold to Commander Charna for one hundred gold."

Kim watched as the she-vorg's hungry gaze caressed her form.

Suddenly another big vorg jumped to his feet, his hairy hand pointing directly at a man, a deep growl rasping his throat. "Blade!"

A stunned silence rained upon the gathering. All eyes followed the pointing hand of the yelling vorg to the spot where a man she would come to know as Arn sat. Men and vorgs scrambled to clear the path between the vorg and Arn, overturning chairs in their rush.

"Blade," the vorg repeated, pulling a folded piece of paper from inside his shirt and spreading it out for all to see. A remarkable likeness of Arn adorned the wanted poster. "Lost favor with your pissant king, did you? No more killing from the shadows. I stand to claim that reward."

Arn remained seated, both feet propped on the table that separated him from the vorg.

The vorg tossed the table aside. Arn landed on his feet before the table hit the floor, his long black blade filling his hand as if it had always been there. His opponent feinted back and forth as he slowly circled Arn. Arn waited, blade down, posture erect.

Noting Arn's stance, the vorg lunged forward, driving his knife toward Arn's stomach.

Arn extended his hands, crossing them right over left in front of his body in a block that stopped the vorgish blade an inch from his chest. He grabbed the vorg's little finger, uncrossing his hands as he did so. A loud crack accompanied the arm's exit from its shoulder socket. The vorg screamed as the knife slipped from his fingers to clatter across the floor.

So intently had Kim watched the fight that she didn't cry out when a slender bowman with dark eyes and a hawkish nose leapt onto the stage, his low voice just loud enough to reach her ears alone.

"If you want freedom, come with me right now."

And as all eyes were locked on the deadly fight opposite the stage, this man slashed her bonds and ushered her out the tavern's back door and up the wooded hillside that skirted the town of Rork, pausing only to cover her with his coat.

—⟋⟍—

Kim blinked as the memory of her dead husband filled her eyes with moisture and threatened to pull a sob from her lips. John was the most tender man she had ever known. His death at the hands of vorgs under Kragan's command had left a jagged hole in her soul, one filled by her necrotic magic. And the erotic longing that this forbidden conjuring unleashed within her focused on Alan. Kim had no illusion that this emotion was love. She would never truly love again.

That did not mean she had ceased being a woman.

But Katrin shared Alan's bed. That knowledge set Kim's teeth on edge. She was angry that such feelings had infected her during their long travels across the Brinje Ocean to Sadamad. By all the gods, Alan was her half brother.

Kim pushed aside the taboo thoughts, burying them under layers of scars. Shifting her eyes to the fogs that surrounded them, she let her strides fall into a rhythm that kept her a few paces behind Alan. Kim would stay close enough to heal this man should he require her magic. She wouldn't repeat the mistake that had cost her husband's life.

—⟋⟍—

Kragan led his company through the Kalnai Mountains, careful to stay well to the east of the harbor of Varjupaik, his magic cloaking their movements. While he'd originally intended to make his way northward to the port city of Vurtsid to retrieve the next of the fingers of amplification, Kragan had changed his mind.

His murder of Varjupaik's merchant queen had allowed Kragan to frame King Godus of Rukkumine for the crime. Thus Kragan had orchestrated the opening salvo of the conflict that doubtless now reigned between the two rival cities. The war would provide just the distraction he needed to obtain the third shard of Landrel's shattered trident from Rukkumine.

Kragan turned to look at the fivescore or more warriors at his command who now trudged along the heavily wooded mountainside. He felt some of them struggling to overcome his will and regain self-control. Unfortunately for them, their efforts were a feeble itch in the back of his mind. The necrotic magic with which he had raised them from the grave bound them to his service. Only death would free them from duty.

5

Alan, his Forsworn company, and the rest of Carol's followers walked out of Galad's time-mists and into the sunny space where time passed at its natural pace. If they could have constantly remained within the rychly mists, they could have made the three-week journey while the same number of days passed in the real world. But Galad needed to periodically dismiss the magical fogs to scout the lands that lay ahead.

With his three inseparable Forsworn companions shadowing his movements, Alan accompanied Arn and Carol to the crest of the ridge while Galad, Kim, and the remainder of the company rested by a stream. Even though Carol summoned an air elemental to mask the group from the sight of others, Alan remained vigilant for ambushes. Kragan might be able to penetrate the cloak.

A light touch on his right shoulder sent a shiver through his body. Kat. Only she would caress him like that. He turned to look into the blue eyes that sparkled like lightning, and for a moment, he felt as if he truly was the Chosen of the Dread Lord. But that thought thrust him back into a past he would have done almost anything to change. Almost.

If Ty hadn't died in his arms on that pinnacle in Areana's Vale, Carol and Kim would have been killed atop that rocky spire. Then the vale would have fallen to Kragan's deep-spawned army of the protectors. Alan reached back and unlimbered the crescent-bladed ax that Ty had handed to him as the Kanjari warrior bled out. Ty's words echoed in Alan's mind.

I'll await you on the other side. When I have made the crossing, let no other touch my ax. I want you alone to use it. You can return it when we meet again. Do I have your word?

Alan's response had been absolute.

You have it.

Now, as the ivory handle rested against his palm, Alan stared at the ax with its rearing stallion etched into the crescent blade, gritted his teeth, and reslung the weapon across his back. He owed the barbarian a debt he would soon repay. Although Arn and Carol both intended to rain their vengeance on Kragan, Alan would remove the wielder's head with Ty's ax.

He felt the gentle touch of long fingers on the back of his neck and smiled at Kat. He looked into eyes that shone with a strange combination of devotion and danger.

By the dark gods, he would wade into the land of the dead for that one look alone.

"Save it for the bedroll," Bill said, bringing a soft chuckle from Quincy.

"What are you nattering about?" Alan asked, immediately regretting that he'd just encouraged the rascal to expound.

"Quincy, was that a fly Kat was brushing from our Chosen's neck?"

"Hard to say, with her leaning in so close. Must have been a gnat."

Hearing Arn and Carol laugh, Alan glared at the two jokesters.

"Keep your mind on the business at hand."

For a moment Bill looked confused. Then his face brightened as if he only now grasped what Alan was referring to.

"Oh . . . the other business."

"Enough," Kat hissed, wheeling on the ranger and swordsman, her hand straying to the hilt of her long knife.

The two took an involuntary step backward, working to stifle their grins.

"Bill," Quincy said, "it seems we accidentally touched a nerve. Perhaps we should give these two some personal space before our dear friend Kat further threatens us."

As the two friends backed off, the look of feigned innocence on Bill's face was so comical that it pulled a reluctant chuckle from Alan, earning him another of Kat's glares. When she turned and walked into the woods, he didn't attempt to stop her. Alan knew that when such a mood was upon his lover, it was best to let Kat work her own way through her emotions.

Rather than stand there alone, Alan moved to the overlook where Arn and Carol gazed northwestward. Several leagues distant, at the far side of a grassy plain, a city spread out along the water, split by a river that emptied into the broad bay.

"So that's where Charna senses Kragan," Alan said.

"Either there," Carol said, "or on one of the ships out on the ocean. She has no feel for how near or far our enemy may be."

"I would expect to see more ships in a harbor as large as that," Arn said, his voice carrying a note of wariness.

Alan felt magic raise the hairs on his forearms as Carol turned the air before them into a mystic far-glass, making the city appear to move much closer. Would he never grow accustomed to the things his sister could do?

He studied the top of the city wall, where sunlight glittered off the shields and armor of soldiers.

"Looks like they expect trouble," Carol said.

"Yes," Arn said. "And across that open space, they'll surely see it coming."

"Well," Carol said, "that's about to be us."

Alan caught his sister's gaze, noted the determination in her brown eyes, and grinned. When they were growing up, she, five years his senior, had always been the cautious one. Over the last couple of years, she had started to embrace a more dangerous approach. It made her all the more appealing.

Alan glanced at the cloudless sky, felt the warmth of the midday sun on his face, and nodded.

"What a lovely day to make trouble."

6

Rukkumine
YOR 415, Mid-Summer

With the sun setting behind him, making his shadow long enough to belong to a normal-size person, Kragan signaled for his company of resurrected heroes to halt and stepped up beside Lieutenant Matas, the man who commanded the raiding party. From this hillside, the sprawling port city of Rukkumine was clearly visible. Only a handful of its ships were anchored in the bay, a sight that Kragan savored. Godus, the city-state's merchant king, had clearly sent his fleet to combat the ships from Varjupaik.

Looking up at his six-foot-tall lieutenant, Kragan gave the command the man expected.

"Prepare my warriors for battle. You will attack the city's northwestern wall at dusk."

Matas scowled but, being subject to Kragan's will, made no objection. He knew that neither he nor any of his men would survive such an assault, even though Kragan would open a breach in the walls. With just over one hundred warriors under his command, they couldn't win against the overwhelming odds Godus would bring to bear against them.

The black-bearded man issued his orders in a baritone voice that captured the attention of every warrior under his command. Kragan didn't bother to watch their preparations. Instead he moved farther up the hillside to a small clearing, isolated from the others by a thick stand of trees.

He seated himself on a flat stone, legs crossed, and lensed the air so that the city seemed to move toward him. From this perch, he studied the layout of the buildings within the city walls. Kragan ignored the palace of the merchant king. Godus held no interest for him. But when his eyes found the turquoise temple of the sea goddess, Dieve, he felt his chest tighten in anticipation. Within those beautiful walls rested another of the sacred altars that one of Landrel's children had built so many centuries ago.

One of the time stones that formed the shrine was special. The cornerstone held at its center another of the tokens of magic amplification that was a remnant of Landrel's Trident.

With his right hand, Kragan pulled the necklace from beneath his shirt to grasp both mummified fingers in his fist. For the brief moment when they were separated from the skin of his chest and not yet within his grasp, Kragan felt weakness leach into his soul. He still maintained his magic, but the loss of its magnification by these two artifacts was worse than physical pain. The absence of their touch pulled a gasp from his lips.

But when his hand closed around them, the rush that filled his head left him ecstatic. How would it feel to add the next token to his collection? Kragan gestured with his left hand, and the pouch slung across his back opened, sending forth the rolled parchment upon which he'd scribed a copy of the *Scroll of Landrel*. From memory he'd re-created the thing in every detail, having summoned a fire elemental to gently burn the words and drawings into the lengthy document. Now it floated before him, unwinding itself from twin rollers to reveal Landrel's masterful drawing of Carol Rafel.

There was no denying the beauty of the witch whom Landrel had prophesied would destroy Kragan. The image of the woman had entranced Kragan for so many centuries that he'd created several statues in her likeness. Like this magical drawing, these replicas were perfect, down to the image of the elemental Jaa'dra branded on her left shoulder.

Kragan had facilitated that branding. He had come oh so close to destroying the wielder who hunted him. But even though she had been a neophyte in her arcane training, she had melted half the face off the body Kragan had once inhabited. *Dangerous* didn't begin to describe Carol Rafel.

He shifted his concentration, sending the twin dowels spinning until the section of text Kragan wanted to see positioned itself for viewing. During his flight into the East, after killing everyone in his birth village, Kragan had solved another cipher hidden within the text of Landrel's prophecy. The time stone he intended to capture in tonight's raid on Rukkumine would dissipate in the coming days, releasing its precious content into this world.

And this one would allow Kragan to use a branch of time magic for which he possessed little talent and against which Carol would have no defense.

Kragan willed the scroll closed, returned it to its waterproof pouch, and rose to his feet just as the sun sank below the western horizon. He walked back to where his soldiers waited, his eagerness growing with each footfall.

—◊◊—

High Priestess Vrajitor knelt before the altar to Dieve, lost in the beauty of the threescore candles atop that time stone dais. She completed her evening prayer that the goddess would grant Rukkumine victory in the struggle to repel the fleet from Varjupaik. When she ended her supplication, she climbed to her feet, her considerable bulk almost making it necessary to supplement her effort with sorcery. Her aquamarine robe billowed around her, its movement magnified by her body's reflection from the polished marble tile floor.

Merchant king Godus's demand for magic wielders to support the warships that set sail to confront the enemy from Varjupaik had reduced the number of the temple's priestly guardians. But the enemy had started this war, so the priesthood had answered its king's call to arms.

Vrajitor spread her arms, summoning the air elemental Nalucire to create the illusion that the deepwater ferns painted onto the blue-green walls swayed in the currents. The peaceful scene brought a smile to her face. No servant of Dieve could love her goddess more than Vrajitor at this moment.

The braying of horns obliterated her serenity. The city walls were under attack, but not from the direction of the harbor. The sound of alarms came from the northwest, an overland assault. Such a raid hadn't occurred during Vrajitor's sixty-one years of life. She couldn't imagine that soldiers from Varjupaik could have made that trek across the southern fringes of the Kalnai Mountains.

With the numbers that that enemy city would have committed to their combat fleet, they must have stripped their own walls of defenders to fight through the lands claimed by the Kalnai mountain clans. The merchant kings and queens of the five harbor cities had long honored the treaty with the clans, and the mountain people would never abide such trespass through their highlands.

Could the declaration of war between Rukkumine and Varjupaik have sparked an attack by the clans, who perhaps saw it as an opportunity to raid, given the city's depleted defenses? That made little sense.

As vicious as were the mountain warriors, the rivalries among the clans would prevent them from forming an alliance capable of confronting Rukkumine's defenders. Even though High Priestess Vrajitor had sent most of her magic-wielding clergy to sea, the two dozen who remained would have little problem overcoming the powers of the few druids available to a single clan. Even the renowned Kalnai chief Vahltehr purportedly had fewer than ten potion-making mistresses to support such a raid.

Vrajitor extracted herself from her reverie, sending forth the magical call that would summon her priests from their prayer booths and here into the central chamber normally reserved for the high priestess at the twilight hour.

Cetaceu was the first of the priests to enter, the bald spot atop his head highlighted by a blond ring. Moments later, the space between the altar and the fifteen-foot-tall double doors was filled with azure-robed priests and their white-gowned acolytes.

The high priestess raised her hands, silencing their low babble.

"Priests, lead your acolytes to the places on the wall where the horns call for help."

"What of the temple?" Cetaceu asked.

"I will remain here to defend it," Vrajitor said, "should it come to that."

The high priestess saw that Cetaceu wanted to argue, but her stern countenance stopped him before he could utter words of caution.

"Begone," she said.

Priests, priestesses, and acolytes made haste to comply with Vrajitor's dictum, and within moments she found herself alone once again. With a wave of her hand, she closed the heavy steel doors and sealed them. Then the air elemental Audra lifted her onto the lofty railing that circled the arches near the temple's highest point.

She stepped past the spiral staircase that provided normal access to this dome-circling walkway, allowing for a glorious view of the entire city. But the unnatural storm clouds that boiled up over the sea to the east unleashed a downpour that sheeted the windows, distorting Vrajitor's perspective. She summoned an earth elemental, dissolving the glass into fine sand. She shifted her attention, sending Audra into the heart of the storm to shred the clouds with cyclonic fury.

A circle of stars appeared over the city. More importantly, the high priestess could now discern the combat along the northwestern wall. She was stunned to see that scores of attackers poured through a room-size hole in the fortifications, where they engaged the city's defenders, who struggled to block the breach.

Sorcery flared along the wall as the priests of Dieve began to assault the enemy. But a mystic shield reflected their magic back into the defenders of the city. Anger coursed through Vrajitor's veins as she directed the cold vise of her mind to pluck more powerful beings from the planes, turning the stone beneath her enemies' feet to thick mud.

But the unknown enemy wielder countered Vrajitor's casting, forcing her to redouble her efforts. A long time had passed since the high priestess last tested her skill's limits. Reaching to the sky, she harnessed her will as never before.

And all around her, the temple groaned.

—⟋⟍—

Kragan redirected the mystic attacks of the priests who assaulted his company. But these clergy-folk were mere minions. Within the heart of the city stood another wielder with arcane talents great enough to pose a threat to him, should he become careless. He needed to focus his attention on dealing with her, but he couldn't allow these lesser priests to destroy his warriors. He couldn't afford to have the city guard descend on him as he contested with a new menace.

He pressed the two mummified fingers that hung around his neck into his flesh, drawing the life force from defenders to fully heal his fighters' wounds. Then Kragan bound a being from each of the four planes to Lieutenant Matas, tasking them to cancel all elemental magic within a hundred paces of the soldier. The binding wouldn't last more than an hour and wouldn't stop the magic wielded by Kragan's elite foe. But Kragan intended to command the high priestess's full attention.

Kragan summoned Uzsleptas, creating a light-refracting bubble of air that would render him invisible to anyone more than two paces away. He concentrated on the power he felt radiating from within the city. Kragan launched himself into the air toward the edifice he knew was the fount of that magic: Rukkumine's Temple of Dieve.

—ɯ—

High Priestess Vrajitor zeroed in on the tendrils of powerful mind magic her adversary used to bind elementals to his will. She followed the strands from the ethereal realms back into the physical world, a name forming as her mind touched his.

Kragan.

Creating a lens of air, she magnified the small form that propelled itself through the twilight sky toward her, a technique she often used to lift herself to her lofty perch. It took impressive talent to control a powerful elemental with precision, that difficulty compounded when vertical and horizontal movements were combined. The feat required tremendous concentration. Any distraction while flying could prove fatal.

A smile tweaked the corners of her lips. Her mighty foe had just made a mistake.

Ball lightning formed between her outstretched hands, then shot outward to explode into the approaching wielder. Vrajitor rained ice shards from the sky, sped by winds that howled like dark-spawn.

The airborne wielder's approach faltered as he shielded himself from the barrage. Floating in the air threescore paces from Vrajitor's temple, the little man was wreathed in electrical arcs. His tawny hair stood straight out, making his sizable head appear enormous.

The river of fire that erupted from Kragan's fingers startled her so that she barely managed to deflect the attack. The flames flowed around Vrajitor to char the beautifully painted ceiling behind her. This sacrilege stoked a fury within her breast and pulled a hiss from her mouth. She hurled roof tiles from nearby buildings at her enemy. One of the hundreds of jagged fragments glanced off Kragan's forehead, opening a satisfying three-inch gash that wept red down the right side of the wielder's face. Kragan snarled and reached inside his leather vest to clutch something she could not see.

Pain blossomed in Vrajitor's right temple, accompanied by a stream of hot blood that stung her eye and blurred her view. But her sight was good enough to observe Kragan's wound knit itself closed as hers opened.

What foul magic was this?

Another of the whirling tiles struck Kragan's side, almost breaking his hold on the air elemental that kept him aloft. The setback was only momentary. A new agony exploded just above Vrajitor's hip, dropping her to her knees on the walkway. She lost concentration. Her multiple attacks faltered.

She erected a mystic shield around her body and, with a supreme burst of will, walled off the torment that threatened to rob her of consciousness. When she refocused her gaze on Kragan, she saw him nod in acknowledgment of a foe who put up a worthy fight. Then he pulled a knife and plunged it into his own thigh.

Vrajitor screamed as she fell, clutching the gushing wound that formed in her left leg. Then Kragan was on the walkway, standing over her. With one great effort she summoned an earth elemental, liquefying the stone of the arch and sending it flowing onto and up Kragan's feet and legs, solidifying as it climbed.

Just as she began to believe she might still win this contest, the high priestess felt Kragan's mind wrest control of the ethereal being she wielded. The stone reliquefied and streamed over her prone form. And in the moments that the flowstone covered her eyes, nose, and mouth, Vrajitor learned the true meaning of terror.

—⁓—

Kragan watched the woman claw at the stone that encased her head. Her legs kicked wildly, then gradually stilled. This round of combat granted him no joy. It sobered him. He had grown overly confident to the extent that this talented priestess came close to knocking him out of the sky. It had been so long since he'd faced a powerful wielder of elemental magic other than Carol Rafel that he had almost forgotten such casters existed.

If this woman, who thought of herself as Vrajitor, had kept some of her lesser priests back at this temple, the high priestess might have defeated him, especially since Kragan had been reckless enough to use an air elemental to fly during combat. Dangerous. Stupid.

He turned away, stepped off the high walkway, and floated to the marble floor sixty feet below. Moving with purpose, he walked to the altar where flames danced atop dozens of candles. He studied the milky-white time stones that the Landrel child had used to build the shrine. There at the lower-right corner was a stone of a considerably darker shade only hours or days from dissipating, just as the *Scroll of Landrel* foretold.

Once again, Kragan summoned Dalg. The earth elemental possessed no power over the white blocks created by Landrel, but it easily dissolved the mortar that cemented the time stones together. Kragan needed only a few moments to pull the cornerstone free. The object was remarkably light. Kragan placed it in his pack alongside the twin dowels containing his copy of Landrel's Scroll.

Then he stood, forced open the magically locked double doors, and stepped out into the night. Instead of repeating his earlier mistake, Kragan distorted the air around him so that he was little more than a ghost moving through the streets and alleys. Staying well to the east of the spot where combat still raged, he reached the northern wall, called upon an earth elemental once more, and stepped through the stone, which acquired the temporary consistency of vapor.

Kragan continued northwest, away from Rukkumine, as quickly as his stubby legs could carry him. His thoughts turned to this latest treasure. If his current interpretation of Landrel's Scroll was correct, the artifact would grant him access to one of the three branches of time magic. Too bad that he would have to wait for Landrel's time stone to dissolve before killing Carol Rafel.

7

Carol stood beside her husband, who'd just finished questioning their she-vorg captive. Although Carol sensed no deceit in Charna's responses, something was clearly bothering Arn.

"What is it that troubles you so?" she asked as they walked back to the head of the column of Alan's warriors.

"I don't know," he said, his eyes locked on the distant city on the far side of the leagues-wide grassy expanse that led to the city's outer wall. "Charna's confidence in the bond between her mind and that of Kragan seems to have become tenuous, as if her sense of direction to the wielder has clouded."

"I didn't see that in her mind."

"Call it a hunch."

Carol came to a stop at the head of the column, where Alan stood alongside Kim and Galad, staring out at the open ground they were about to cross. Movement in the sky attracted her gaze. A hawk soared high above, circling as it hunted. Perfect.

Carol linked minds with the bird of prey, assaulted by its hunger and bloodlust. The ground sped away below her as she redirected the hawk toward the city. She stayed high, making expert use of the air currents to propel herself toward the wall and the edifices it protected. The guardsmen who manned the wall wore chain-and-leather armor, their shields emblazoned with a merchant ship on an azure sea. All men, these soldiers gave no indication that they saw the company that would soon make its way out onto the plain beyond the walls.

As she soared above the city, Carol watched as people moved along wide streets and narrow alleys to gather in the marketplace set up in the expansive central square. On the north side of the market area, a coliseum or amphitheater rose, its thousands of bench seats empty. She looked down at the people engaged in trade, their clothing a kaleidoscope of colors.

A short distance west of the central square, an ivory-domed building towered above the surrounding buildings. But the westward-facing wall lay crumbled, massive stones spread across the street that led toward the port. Many workers moved on scaffolding, working to repair the damage to the temple.

Carol winged her way westward to the harbor. She spotted several sailors, both men and women, all wearing loose-fitting blouses tucked into tight black trousers and tall crimson boots. She was surprised by how few ships were in the harbor. Many piers speared out from this seaport, indicative of robust merchant shipping activity. But on this day only three ships sat moored. A closer look revealed that each of the vessels was under repair from what appeared to be combat damage. No wonder people were jumpy.

She made the full transition back to her own body.

"Remember," Carol said to Alan, "our approach to the city gates must be made in a casual, nonthreatening posture."

Alan rolled his shoulders, making the crescent blade of the ax strapped across his back cast the sun's reflection across her face. He raised his voice and issued the command to his Forsworn.

"Forward, but keep it slow and easy."

Carol watched the twoscore warriors who made their unhurried way out onto the thigh-deep grassland, their shaved heads glistening in the sun. Despite the leisurely pace at which the double columns followed Princess Kimber and Prince Galad, they couldn't shed their air of danger. She walked at Arn's side, having positioned herself a few paces behind Kim and Galad, who sported the resplendent aquamarine uniforms of Endarian royalty.

Queen Elan had sent the royal garb for precisely this purpose. Kim and Galad would present themselves as emissaries of Endar, bringing word of the dissipation of the time-mists that had isolated the Endarian Continent from the rest of the world for the last four centuries. They would present the queen's gift and express Elan's eagerness to reestablish the trade relationships of old.

Assuming that they and their company weren't immediately arrested. But even if that eventuality came to pass, Carol had given instructions that no one resort to violent action. Patience was to be the watchword.

"If Kragan is within those walls," Arn said, "he may have corrupted the city's rulers, just as he did within the kingdom of Tal."

Carol considered and rejected this line of thought. "That process took Kragan years to accomplish. He just fled from our last encounter. I doubt that he'll dare to directly confront me before he acquires several fragments of Landrel's shattered trident."

"And if he's more aggressive than you think?"

"Then I will destroy him."

—⁓—

King Trgovec, having risen to the throne of Varjupaik after the murder of Queen Lielisks, looked up to see a green-robed female sage stride rapidly toward the throne. Three paces from where he sat, she dropped to one knee and bowed.

"Rise, Kurirka. What news brings you to me?"

"My king, an unusual caravan approaches from the Kalnai foothills."

Trgovec straightened in surprise.

"Kalnai clansmen?"

"No, Highness. The group numbers just over twoscore. They are heavily armed but show no signs of aggression. They are led by two people with darker skin than that of our people, just as described in the old tomes. The man and woman wear the regal dress of the lost realm of Endar."

The utterance pulled Trgovec to his feet, heart thumping.

"Take me to the eastern wall," he said, his voice hoarse with excitement. "I must behold these foreigners with my own eyes."

Trgovec signaled to one of his personal guards, a fist of whom were always near his side.

"Summon my carriage."

"Yes, Highness."

The guard turned and jogged from the room, her chain mail shirt rattling against the hilt of her curved sword.

When Trgovec and his scribe climbed down from the carriage near the city's east gate, a burly, black-bearded captain stepped forward and thumped his right hand to his breastplate in salute.

"Captain, show me the caravan that approaches my city."

The man turned and led Trgovec and Kurirka up the switchback staircase that provided access to the top of the wall. After three dozen steps, the merchant king paused for breath, his heart pounding within his rotund torso. But when he began climbing again, such was his eagerness that he made it all the way to the top without taking another break.

The captain stepped onto the turret positioned above the barred steel gates. At first Trgovec failed to see anything beyond the cropland that lay fallow. The captain pulled forth a far-glass, handed it to the king, and pointed toward the foothills several leagues to the southeast.

Trgovec swept the magnifying device back and forth, spotted something, and leaned against a merlon to steady the tremor that crept into his hands. A double line of armored soldiers marched directly toward him, most of them pale of skin and bald of head. At the forefront of these strode a warrior of massive frame. The king carefully adjusted his view to focus on the two apparent Endarians who led the entire assemblage, both dressed in formfitting blue-green uniforms that shimmered in the sunlight. The tall male's skin was a shade darker than that of the female who strode at his side, but hers was still of a deeper tone than Trgovec's olive complexion.

Kurirka's description proved accurate. The pair resembled the drawings of the Endarians with whom the five seaport city-states of Sadamad had once conducted extensive trade. That commerce had ended four centuries ago when the mysterious time-mists sealed off the Endarian Continent.

Trgovec shifted the far-glass up just a bit. Behind these two leaders, Trgovec saw another couple. The woman wore a uniform that shifted colors to blend with her background. But the man who walked beside her wore all black, with knives strapped to his thighs and sheathed in his boots. A larger blade was strapped to his side.

The menacing group approached the walled city with such an apparent lack of concern that the sight startled the king. If they wanted to pique Trgovec's curiosity, they had succeeded.

He turned to his captain.

"Ready your archers, but do *not* attack the travelers. I will judge whether to allow any of them to enter when they arrive."

"Yes, Majesty."

Trgovec once again trained the far-glass on the caravan. Long before he became king, he had made his vast fortune by risking what others were unwilling to venture. Now, in keeping with his nature, he would see what these foreigners wanted to offer.

Handing the far-glass back to the captain, the king led Kurirka down the stairs to his carriage. He would await these strangers from the comfort of its lush interior.

—⁂—

As the caravan approached the closed city gates, Arn watched the archers form along the crenels atop the city wall. They were joined by a handful of people in blue robes, priests or magic wielders from the look of them. Galad and Kim maintained their steady pace, showing no signs of concern. Although he didn't glance back at Alan and his Forsworn, Arn didn't doubt that they mirrored the attitude of the Endarian royals.

When Kim and Galad reached a point a dozen paces from the thirty-foot-tall steel gates, Galad raised his good right fist, bringing the company behind him to a halt. His stentorian voice echoed off the high wall.

"Hail, guardians of the gate."

One of the olive-skinned soldiers atop the wall leaned out from a turret above the closed portal to the city.

"State your business, stranger."

"I am Prince Galad. My sister, Princess Kimber, and I come as emissaries of our mother, Queen Elan of Endar. The time-mists around our continent have been breached."

"What proof have you of this claim?"

"Queen Elan desires to reestablish the profitable trading relationships between the kingdom of Endar and the city-states of Sadamad. We bear a royal gift for your ruler, a token of our mother's goodwill."

The soldier didn't reply. Instead he disappeared back inside the turret. For an interval that stretched into minutes, the guards left the company standing where they halted. Arn could sense the tension building among the archers atop the battlements, but they didn't draw back their bows, inaction that he took as a positive sign.

When the twin gates opened, they swung inward with barely a squeal of metal on metal. Arn watched as the man who had challenged them from atop the wall strode forward, accompanied by fourteen guardsmen. He brought his contingent to a halt five paces in front of Kim and Galad.

"Prince Galad and Princess Kimber, King Trgovec invites you to an evening feast in celebration of your arrival. You two will stay the night. The rest of your caravan must remain outside these gates pending the outcome of tomorrow's discussions. You must also leave your weapons here."

"Agreed," Galad said.

Without hesitation Galad drew his sword and handed it to Arn. Kim spread her hands to show that she was unarmed.

Arn had speculated that the demand to disarm would be a pre-condition for meeting the city's monarch. But he didn't like the idea of Galad and Kim entering the city alone, not knowing if Kragan was also within those walls.

At Galad's signal, Quincy Long strode forward to hand the prince one of five emerald-green bags that contained the royal gifts that Queen Elan had sent with them. When Galad turned toward the city, the twin gates parted with a gentle squeal, a testament to their well-oiled hinges. Arn watched his two Endarian friends stride forward to be met by the soldier.

"I am Captain Mecevalec. I will escort you to our palace."

As a squad of guards formed ranks behind them, the group passed into the city. With a loud clank, the gates closed behind them. For a moment Arn debated setting Slaken aside to exercise his time-sight, but he immediately discarded the notion.

He wouldn't willingly embrace the loss of self-control.

Alan's command pulled him out of his reverie.

"Make camp."

Turning away from the gate, Arn walked with Carol into the center of the perimeter that Alan's Forsworn moved to establish. Selecting a comfortable spot, Carol seated herself in cross-legged fashion, closed her eyes, and entered the deep state of meditation that she had long ago mastered.

A dozen paces away, one of Alan's Forsworn stood watch over Charna, having chained the she-vorg's hands and ankles together so that she couldn't stand. As soon as they found Kragan, Arn would have no more need of her.

As if sensing his thoughts, Charna met his gaze, her lips curling into a combination of a snarl and a grin. Arn understood that look. She was as anxious to bring about the meeting of Kragan and Arn as he was.

Arn turned to watch the scarlet fire of sunset paint the sky over the seaport city. If Kragan was within those walls, was he hidden or welcome? Although Arn's intuition denied the likelihood of the latter, he still worried about Kim and, to a lesser extent, Galad.

Taking a deep breath, he shoved aside the negative thoughts and began spreading the bedrolls near Carol. Facing his wife, he seated himself on the blankets. As twilight surrendered the night sky to the gibbous moon, he continued to watch her, longing for the serenity that he saw in her lovely face.

But as he ran his fingers over Slaken's runed haft, Arn knew that on this night he had no hope of achieving a peaceful state of mind.

—⚭—

Within the palace, Kim's room lay across the hall from Galad's. Having used the washbasin to refresh herself, she walked over and knocked on her brother's door. With sunset's arrival, the time for someone to escort them to the feasting hall was almost at hand.

Galad opened the door and allowed her to enter.

Kim moved to the end table atop which the emerald bag rested and placed her hand on the soft cloth that covered Queen Elan's royal gift. As she stared down at the token of her mother's goodwill, Galad placed his hand on her shoulder. She turned to look up at him, seeing in his eyes a tenderness that she almost never observed in her brother. Kim had always looked up to her serious and driven sibling, thirteen years her senior. Although she knew that he cared deeply for her, Galad made a habit of hiding his emotions. Now he allowed something to penetrate that gruff exterior.

"What's wrong?" she asked.

"That's precisely what I was going to ask you."

"I don't understand."

"You're changing."

"I've lost my father and two of the men who rescued and befriended me. One of them was my husband. What do you expect?"

Galad's eyes narrowed, his focus on her intensifying as he appeared to carefully weigh his words.

"Your grief saddens me as well, but I'm not referring to that."

"Then what?"

"In Endar Pass, when you violated Mother's edict that forbade the use of necrotic magic, I saw something in your face that disturbed me. I thought that in the heat of the battle, my impression was wrong."

Kim felt her temples throb as she strove to tamp down her rising anger.

"You," she said, thrusting her finger close to her brother's nose, "are the one who pushed me into breaking that law."

"I saw that look again aboard the *Saimniece*, when we battled the sea creatures."

"And what look is that?"

"Ecstasy."

A knock at the door drew Kim's attention. She struggled to compose herself as Galad's stoic mask reasserted itself. With an effort she shoved the argument into a shadowed corner of her mind.

"Enter," Galad said.

The door opened to admit Captain Mecevalec.

"The feast awaits you," he said. "King Trgovec has reserved two places of honor at his side."

Kim and Galad followed the captain down two long hallways richly adorned with tapestries portraying merchant ships overflowing with goods and treasure. By the time she reached the end of that hall, Kim had restored the calm with which she wanted to meet the king. But the feast chamber took her by surprise.

A thirty-foot ceiling graced the room, with painted images of sailing ships on the high seas. The walls were covered in more intricately stitched tapestries. Guards stood at attention along its walls, spaced two paces apart, but there was a complete absence of furniture.

Instead a forty-foot-by-ten-foot rug lay stretched out in the room's center, its length covered in trays heaped with wide flatfish and spiny, ten-legged shelled creatures. Baskets of bread and dishes piled high with thick stalks covered in yellow buds dripped butter. Three dozen colorfully dressed men and women sat on pillows with large plates and no silverware in front of them. Servants, dressed in gray, continued to add to the cornucopia.

The heavyset man she took for the king sat alone at the far end of the rug with an empty place on each side of him. He waved them forward, so Kim and Galad made their way down the line and took their seats.

"Welcome, my friends," he said to each of the siblings, pressing his right palm to his heart, a motion that Kim and then Galad mirrored.

"We have many important matters to discuss," Galad said.

"Tonight, we eat and drink," King Trgovec said. "I will not discuss business until we have supped together. It is our way."

"Good," Kim said. "This food smells wonderful."

"Wait until you taste our tekocine. It warms the belly and lightens the head. Be forewarned."

The king grabbed one of the multilegged spiny creatures from one platter along with several red and orange vegetables from another. He ripped off a leg, cracked it in half, and sucked out its meaty center. The rest of the diners immediately followed his example. Kim hesitated, then began heaping food onto her plate.

If not for the months she'd spent in the wilds with John, Arn, and Ty, Kim would have been reluctant to get her hands greasy with food. Nevertheless, the way these people practically buried their faces in the sumptuous fare made her uncomfortable. The servants busied themselves, bringing bowls of clean water for each guest so they could periodically wash their hands.

As Kim ate she observed Trgovec. Beneath his jovial manner lurked a keen wit and the heart of a wolf. She found herself liking the man, despite the growing evidence that he would be a challenging bargaining partner.

The king's warning about the tekocine proved accurate. As Kim raised the small glass of alcohol to her lips, the fumes burned her nostrils, then made her want to sneeze. Rather than suffer that indignity, she pulled a trickle of life magic from a young man in a bright orange-and-green shirt, exchanging her sneeze for his comfort.

"Ha," King Trgovec said. "I thought you took your draft with more ease than that, Krmar."

The laughter from those around the king's target brought a flush to the fellow's face that made Kim want to apologize. Despite catching a knowing look from her brother, Kim held her tongue.

As Trgovec predicted, the strong drink lightened Kim's manner such that, by the end of the meal, she found herself chatting with the large man as if she had known him for years. Although she could have removed the alcohol's effects on her brain, she chose not to.

How long had it been since she felt this lighthearted? Princess Kimber raised her glass high.

"To King Trgovec. Thank you for this most wonderful meal. And to the renewal of the ancient trading alliance between Endar and Varjupaik."

The king lifted his drink, his eyes narrowing as he reappraised her. "May our relationship be mutually beneficial."

—ɯ—

The cave that Kragan's magic had carved into the face of the cliff sealed itself after he entered. A circle of dancing lights, reminiscent of candle flames, surrounded the spot where he sat on the granite floor, leaning over the time stone that had changed from off-white to gray. His heart pounded, and he rubbed his hands together and then turned his palms outward as one would to receive a fire's warmth on a frigid winter's day.

It took almost an hour for the brick to dissolve into a mist that Kragan didn't dare touch lest it injure his hand. But when that fog cleared, the mummified thumb that lay on the stone ended his hesitation. Kragan placed it in his palm, feeling a coolness spread up his arm as an entirely different magical channel opened within him.

Kragan tightened his fist around this third fragment from Landrel's Trident. Having made a detailed study of the nine magics during the thousands of years of his life, Kragan knew what he wanted to do with the new power the object granted him. But even though he understood the theory of channeling time magic, he'd never practiced it, which posed an obstacle to its effective use. Worse, if he attempted to wield too much of the magic, his lack of control could backfire on him. Best to start small.

He selected two of the arcane flames that formed the circle around him, establishing two tiny channels, letting the darker rychly mist form around the rightmost of these candles while a balancing quantity of white pomaly mist shrouded the one to his left. Satisfied with this minor success, Kragan intensified both flows.

Midnight came and went as Kragan experimented. Since no elemental magic could pass through the boundary of where time flowed at a different rate, each flame he targeted winked out of existence.

Kragan ended his practice session and restored his flame circle, convinced that he could control enough time-mist to kill Carol Rafel. He didn't need to age her entire body. If he could send concentrated rychly tendrils flowing through her eyes and into her brain, he could end the threat she posed. But to do that, he needed to see Carol.

That would not be a problem.

He took several slow breaths, acquiring the calm state of mind that allowed him to achieve total concentration. Then he enabled his mental connection to Charna, the pain from her cramped muscles blossoming in his mind as he forced her to open her eyes.

She lay with hands and ankles chained as the moon bathed the camp in its pale light. She looked at Carol Rafel sitting in meditation mere paces from the spot where Charna lay bound. Blade stood watch over Carol, facing the city wall.

Kragan's elation threatened to break his concentration. With a flick of his will, he snatched Lwellen from the realm of air, spraying sand toward Carol. As he had known would happen, Carol's eyes popped open as she parried the attack. Her angry gaze shifted to Charna as Kragan wielded the time magic, creating a white ball of pomaly mist even as a thin spear of rychly mist flowed into Carol's eyes.

Her scream pulled a snarl from Charna's dripping jowls. But as Kragan intensified his channeling, Blade blurred into motion. A dagger sprouted from Charna's chest, sending a river of pain across their mental link and into Kragan. Charna's eyes shifted from Carol to the lunging assassin. Her last sight was of the man's black knife cutting an arc toward her throat, driven with enough force to cut Charna's head from her body.

Kragan jerked as his connection to the she-vorg died. The brilliant burst of agony that accompanied the knife as it slashed through her spine almost robbed Kragan of his consciousness. He found himself lying faceup on the cold stone of the cave floor, panting from sudden terror. Working to still his trembling hands, one of which still clutched the token of time magic, Kragan rolled to his knees. For endless moments he remained there.

The summoned flame circle went out, leaving him in darkness so thick he could taste it. He was completely drained, unable to cast even a minor spell to drive back the black curtain that draped him.

Had he killed Carol Rafel?

Kragan recalled the sound of her scream, full of agony, but with no trace of a death rattle. And now she was beyond his reach. Thank the deep for that. The weakness that left him unable to stand gradually curled him into a ball on the cold stone. Lying there, he let fatigue carry him into the land of dreams.

—ᴍ—

Sensing danger, Arn spun to see smoke curl from Charna's moonlit fingers and spear toward Carol. The throwing dagger departed his left hand as he heard Carol's wail. He closed the distance to the she-vorg in an instant. His right hand slashed Slaken into Charna's neck, powered by such a combination of terror and rage that the blade cut through muscle, tendon, and spine in a single blow, sending the severed head rolling away from Charna's prone body.

Arn raced to where Carol lay on her back, moaning, palms pressed to her eyes. He dropped to his knees beside her, gently placing his hands atop hers.

"Let me look at the wound," he said, trying to purge the quaver from his voice.

Ever so slowly he pulled her hands away from her face. Carol stared upward toward the brilliant moon.

What he saw froze his heart. Her rich brown eyes had gone milky white, as if they'd aged a hundred years.

"Gods help me," she whispered. "I'm blind."

—⚏—

"Kim, wake up," Galad said, shaking her. "A messenger has come from the east gate."

"What is wrong?"

"Carol has been grievously injured. Perhaps your life magic can help her."

Having slept in her clothes, Kim threw off her covers, slid into her boots, and followed Galad out into the hall, where the herald of these bad tidings awaited alongside King Trgovec.

"Word came of your half sister's wounding. My driver will escort you to my carriage, which awaits you in the courtyard. Make haste."

Kim hurried down the hall after the charioteer, uncaring that Galad remained behind. She climbed into the carriage as the driver scrambled up to take the reins. With a yell and a crack of the whip, he put the team of horses into a fast trot along the empty, moonlit streets. When the king's driver brought the carriage to a halt before the city's eastern gates, Kim waited just long enough for him to have them opened before leaping out. She ran through the opening and raced toward the spot where Alan stood, his face grim.

"Take me to her," Kim said.

Alan led her into the encampment to the place where Carol lay on the ground, her head resting on a rolled blanket. Arn knelt by her side, head bowed, holding her hand.

Kim dropped to her knees beside her sister.

"I am here."

"Her eyes," Arn said.

When Kim placed her palm gently on her sister's forehead, Carol opened her eyelids. Kim barely managed to stifle the gasp that despair tried to pry from her lips. The sight of Carol's milky-white eyes made the situation clear. Kim's life magic couldn't reverse aging, and those eyes were as old as any she had ever seen.

"Time magic," she said, squeezing Carol's hand. "I'm so sorry, but this wounding is beyond my art to undo."

When Carol closed her eyes again, tears cut trails down her cheeks.

Arn grabbed his black knife and drove it hilt deep into the dirt. Releasing Slaken, he lay down next to Carol, pulling her into his arms so that her head rested on his chest. Kim had never seen Arn cry, but now, as his hand lightly stroked Carol's cheek, he sobbed unashamedly.

Kim climbed to her feet, needing to get away from this tragic scene, away from her guilt at being incapable of healing her sister. Feeling as if all the strength had been siphoned from her body, she stumbled into Alan. He swept her into his strong arms. He offered no words of consolation. He merely enfolded her in an embrace that sapped her desire to be alone.

She clung to him, relying on his strength to keep her upright. His arms held her so close that she could feel the thumping of his heart. Or was it her heart hammering with such vigor? How could she allow lust into her mind while her half sister lay blinded and weeping a few dozen paces away? When Alan released her, Kim almost failed to do the same. She took a deep breath, then turned and walked back toward the waiting carriage.

As she exited the camp in the pale moonlight, Kim met Katrin's gaze. The woman's blue eyes bored into her with an unspoken accusation that the Endarian's pursed lips confirmed. Kim walked on by, feeling that harsh glare all the way back into the city.

—◊◊◊—

Finally Carol slept. Arn carefully extracted himself from her arms, settling her head on a bedroll. He grabbed Slaken. The knife he'd held precious for so many years was now anathema to him. He silently made his way across the encampment to the place where the two bags filled with cooking implements were stored. Fumbling inside the first of them, he found the large skillet.

Then he walked out through the guarded perimeter, heading away from the city. No guard sought to question him. That was fortunate. Arn was immersed in a mood so foul that he doubted he could have controlled the hostile response that any delay would have pulled from him.

Carol's injury was his fault. How many times had she asked him to put Slaken aside and embrace his time-sight? In his dreams of Landrel, the long-dead wielder urged him to rid himself of the blade. What had Landrel said to Arn about Slaken?

Because you are also of the talent, I cannot foresee which choice you will make with that mystic artifact. But know this. It is your salvation. It is the destruction of all you shall ever love. Only you can determine which of those futures you will embrace.

But because Slaken blocked mind magics, including the summoning of elementals, Arn had stubbornly clung to the runed knife, believing it would enable him to exact his vengeance on Kragan. Instead Slaken had prevented Arn from seeing the horrible events about to transpire.

A hundred paces east of the encampment, Arn seated himself on the ground and placed the skillet between his legs. He switched Slaken to his left hand. Then he extended his right hand over the pan and pressed the tip of the blade into his palm, cutting a two-inch slash. The pain lanced up his arm, but Arn welcomed it.

He dropped the knife into the skillet and let his blood pour down over the runed handle, just as he had seen in another of his dreams. The glyphs drank the blood with a thirst. A mist arose from the pan, giving the knife a ghostly appearance. And as the runes consumed their fill, they gradually disappeared, releasing the four elementals that the glyphs bound within the haft.

Light-headed, Arn studied the pan's contents. The knife handle was gone, leaving behind the blade and a bloody wooden shard.

Not a piece of wood. A skeletal center finger.

Having seen the drawings of the nine mummified fingers within the *Scroll of Landrel*, Arn knew he was now looking at one of them. He'd carried the knife all these years, not knowing that one of the world's most magical artifacts was hidden inside its haft. Arn blinked. Of all the incredible ways that Landrel had manipulated the lives of people, this seemed the most unlikely. He was certain that the ancient master of the nine magics was toying with him.

Arn squeezed his right fist to stanch the flow of blood. He considered grabbing the artifact from the pan, but the visions such a thought spawned in his tired mind dissuaded him. So he climbed back to his feet, grabbed the skillet by the handle, and carried it back into camp, ignoring the curious looks from the Forsworn perimeter guards.

When he reached the spot where Carol slept, Arn set the bloody pan on the ground, its mystic contents undisturbed. Wrung out, he cut a strip from his blanket, bound his wounded hand, and settled in beside his wife. With grief gnawing at his gut, his voice was a mere whisper.

"Ah, my love. Forgive me."

8

Varjupaik
YOR 415, Mid-Summer

Carol awoke to a splitting headache. Feeling the sun on her face, she opened her eyes. She didn't see blackness, just a void lacking variation or color. The sun warmed her cheeks, yet a chill formed in the sockets that housed her sightless orbs. But the smells of flowers, grass, and unwashed bodies overwhelmed her.

The memory of last night flooded into her consciousness, causing her to sit up straight.

"I'm here, my love," Arn said.

She felt him take her hand in both of his, but she jerked it from his grasp. She tried to speak, but the constriction in her throat stopped her. To have her eyesight stolen from her seemed so unfair. Carol couldn't get a handle on her emotions, oscillating among sadness, anger, and self-pity. She'd always thought of herself as so resilient. What a deep-spawned lie that had turned out to be. Now she was punishing the man she loved above all else.

Carol took a shuddering breath and tried again. "I'm sorry."

"Don't be. I deserved that."

"No. My head hurts, and I'm thirsty."

"Sit still. I'll bring a waterskin."

In moments Arn returned to her side, guiding her hand to the mouthpiece. Carol tilted it to her lips, drinking her fill of the soothing liquid. Then she poured water into her hand and splashed it onto her face and eyes. She returned the flask to her husband and felt his arms encircle her.

Self-pity. She despised that as the ultimate sign of weakness. What would her mentor Hawthorne say if he could see how she was dealing with this adversity? He would tell her to get off her butt and master the situation within which she found herself.

Furious, Carol did exactly that.

She climbed to her feet, stood tall, and reached out to touch Arn's chest. She traced her way down both arms to take his hands in hers. She couldn't see him, but through her touch she could feel his mind. Carol forged her mental link to her husband, feeling him acknowledge their connection. As she looked through Arn's eyes, the image of herself formed in her mind. His sorrow was palpable, but she sensed no revulsion as he stared into her face.

Carol's eyes were cloudy white marbles. But her chin no longer quivered, and the set of her jaw showed her newfound resolve. Not exactly beautiful, but a look she could learn to live with. The throbbing in her temples made her legs unsteady, and she sat back down on her blanket, allowing Arn to help her sit.

Although he didn't wince, she felt the pain that lanced through his right hand. Then she spotted the bloodstained skillet and the knife blade that lay within it.

"What?"

"Last night, I destroyed it, just as Landrel showed me."

Her heartbeat jumped as the meaning within those words hit her.

"Slaken?"

"Yes. My thirst for that knife almost killed you. It cost you your sight."

"That wasn't your fault."

"Wasn't it? If I'd done as you asked and as Landrel tried to tell me, I might have foreseen the attack on you. I could have prevented it."

Arn picked up the pan and knelt beside her. His gaze focused on a smaller object than the blade. A skeletal appendage. The knowledge of what she was seeing stunned her.

"That was hidden within Slaken's haft," Arn said.

"A shard from Landrel's Trident!"

"In my dream Landrel was clutching a finger just like this one."

"You haven't touched it?"

"It could make me lose my way back to reality."

"Landrel's Scroll says the bones must directly touch a wielder's skin to function. We should get a cloth, clean it up, keep it safe."

Arn looked at her, reaching out his uninjured hand to caress her cheek.

"I can feel your headache and exhaustion. Rest. I'll take care of the artifact."

His words pulled Carol back to an awareness of her own condition, confirming the truth of his words. She lay back, resting her head on a rolled blanket. Then a fresh wave of fatigue broke her connection to Arn's mind.

Carol closed her eyes.

—∿—

King Trgovec sat atop his throne, staring at the two Endarian royals with whom he'd engaged in negotiations for the last two hours. They'd presented him with a gift that befitted his station, one that whispered of the treasures that would await the merchant king who struck up the first trading relationship with the people from the Endarian Continent.

The solid gold dagger's hilt was inlaid with precious stones that were extremely rare on Sadamad.

Still, the gift he wanted most stood before him, her luxuriant hair framing a face that would fill the sea goddess with envy. Trgovec lusted for other women. As king, he could have his pick. But this princess exuded a mysterious, supernatural aura that enthralled him. And there was a sadness in her mahogany eyes that bespoke tragic loss and unquenchable longing.

Trgovec figured that, given time, his wit and will could coax happiness from the princess. Once more, he marveled at how this woman affected him. Far more than her physical beauty was at work. His advisers would have no doubt told him that his excitement and attraction were side effects of the thrill associated with cementing control of this most valuable of trade routes. He mulled over the idea and rejected it. No. This was something primal.

But Trgovec hadn't become the most successful merchant in Sadamad by exposing the breadth and depth of his desires to his negotiating partners. The question was how to get the princess to stay here in Varjupaik.

"Varjupaik must be the principal trading partner to the kingdom of Endar," he bellowed. "It is imperative that ships from any of our sister city-states bear a letter of authorization, marked with my seal, to trade with your people."

"For which you will levy a significant tax," Kim said.

"Clearly."

"These terms will not be palatable to Sadamad's other merchant kings and queens," Galad said.

"That is the value in being the deal's architect."

"And you agree to our terms?" Kim asked.

"With one minor caveat."

"Which is?" Galad asked.

"That Princess Kimber remain in Varjupaik as Endar's ambassador to my royal court. In return I will place fifty of my soldiers under Prince Galad's command to serve as an escort during your journey to the merchant kingdoms of Vurtsid, Jogi, and Paradiis. I will also provide wagons stocked with food and supplies. Unfortunately, due to the state of war that exists between Varjupaik and Rukkumine, I cannot spare any ships to take you by sea."

"This is too much of a departure from our agreement," Galad said. "My sister is my equal in rank, and her talents are crucial to our mission's success."

"Then it seems we've come to an impasse."

"Perhaps another of your sister city-states will find greater value in our offer," Kim said.

"One hundred soldiers, wagons, and supplies for your journey."

"No," Galad said.

"Godus, the merchant king of Rukkumine, has sent raiding parties into the southern Kalnai Mountains. You may need the extra security I tender."

"We will take our chances."

Trgovec fought to keep his emotions in check.

"What? Have you no counteroffer?"

Prince Galad started to speak, but Kim held up her hand, cutting him off.

"If you will allow my caravan into your city and provide accommodations while we prepare for our journey, I will agree to remain in Varjupaik as Queen Elan's ambassador to your court."

Trgovec clapped his hands.

"Excellent."

"But," Kim said, "only after we complete the mission my mother assigned us. Once we have accomplished our goal and met with the other merchant kings and queens, I will fulfill my part of our bargain."

Not exactly what Trgovec had hoped for. Then again, delayed gratification was far superior to failure.

"My scribe will draw up the treaty."

"One last matter," Kim said. "On our way here, we were attacked by a dangerous wielder. At the throat of a large bay a few dozen leagues southwest of here, the mage massacred a fishing village of several hundred people."

"Survivors?"

"We found only the bones of men, women, and children. They were little people."

"The Zvejys people of Klampyne were my subjects. Describe this wielder."

"We only saw the results of his magic. But we believe that he was also responsible for last night's attack that blinded my half sister."

"You are sure this is a man?"

"We believe so."

"If this wielder has somehow slipped into my city, my priests will find the beast and drag him here to face my justice."

"Have care," Galad said. "He wields an extremely powerful dark magic."

"I have more than enough priests to handle one foul mage, no matter how formidable."

"This wielder is different," Kim said. "His abilities go beyond what you can imagine."

"I will share your warning with my clergy."

"Then Galad and I will return to our company to inform them of our agreement."

"I will send word once accommodations are ready to receive them."

Trgovec watched as the Endarian prince and princess strode from his throne room, feeling a tremendous sense of satisfaction burn away his anger. Not only had he placed Varjupaik in charge of all trade between the continents of Endar and Sadamad, but he had also laid the foundation for formalizing the bond between his kingdom and that of Queen Elan.

And in doing so he would elevate Kimber from princess to queen.

—⟋ꟷ—

Arn cleaned the caked blood from the shard of Landrel's Trident with a damp cloth, careful not to let the thing touch his skin. He was having a hard time fighting off the visions that threatened to whisk him from this reality into possible futures that branched away from it. To have his untrained time-sight thus augmented would be to succumb to madness.

Once he judged the finger clean, he placed it within a little pouch that he strapped to his belt. Without Slaken in the sheath at his side, he felt naked, vulnerable. Although he could carve a new haft for the blade he'd retrieved when he washed out the skillet, it would no longer protect him from magic. Nevertheless, he slid the steel cutting edge back into its leather scabbard, noting the hiss it made as it slid home.

The sound of leather brushing metal wasn't loud, but it brought Carol's eyes open. She reached out with her left hand, feeling for him.

Arn reached out to meet her grasp, watching as relief flooded her face. He helped her to her feet.

"I dreamed that I lost you," she said.

"Never going to happen."

"The loss of my sight greatly decreases my value in our fight against Kragan."

"No. You can see through my eyes or through your mental control of animals."

"I can't make a bond without touching you."

"I've contemplated this. That's true for the first link. Once you can look through my sight, you can then hop to another host as usual."

She paused to consider this.

"But in the past, I could connect to a distant bird and still maintain an awareness of my own surroundings. Now, my body will be completely helpless while I perform such a distant connection."

"Not if you retain a partial channel to me while I remain close to you."

"I need you to wield your own talents against Kragan."

"I'm your husband."

"You are not my caretaker. I will find my way."

With frustration threatening to escalate their talk into an argument, Arn looked around to see Kim and Galad approaching. Kim walked directly to Carol, threw her arms around her sister, and hugged her. For several moments they clung to each other. Neither woman shed a tear.

"I'm all right," Carol said, releasing Kim. "What news do you and Galad bring?"

"I have much to tell."

"Then," Arn said, "I propose that you tell it while we eat. Carol has had nothing since yesterday."

The meal consisted of their standard travel rations: dried and salted meat, flatbread, and water. Arn was pleased to see that Carol attacked the food as ravenously as he did. And as they ate, Kim and Galad spoke of their negotiations with King Trgovec and of his promise to have his priests scour the city for any sign of Kragan.

"If they find him," Carol said, "I'll sense the fireworks."

Arn suddenly found himself swept away in a new vision that happened too fast to block, and because Carol's mind was connected to his, she was hurled into the dream right alongside him.

—⚌—

Carol watched as guards and a blue-robed woman escorted a small man into a regally appointed chamber. An elegant woman with olive skin and auburn hair sat atop a gold throne in an azure gown. Carol had no substance, observing the proceedings as a phantasm.

The escorted party stood only as tall as the lead guardsman's belt. His tawny head, hands, and feet seemed large for such a diminutive body.

"Queen Afacere," said the woman whom Carol took to be a priest. "This Zvejys man claims to carry word of marauders from across the Brinje Ocean."

"And you thought his words important enough to bring him before me?"

"Not his words, Highness. I thought you should see the evidence he showed me."

The queen turned her attention from the priest to the tiny man.

His face filled with sorrow, he dropped to one knee and bowed his head.

"What is your name?" the queen asked.

"I am Kragan, Klampyne Village's wielder of magic and the sole survivor of a massacre. Vicious marauders from across the sea have made me the last of the Zvejys race."

His words stunned Carol. She felt Arn react just as strongly.

"Rise, Kragan, and prove to me the truth of what you say."

"Yes, Majesty."

Kragan stood, furrowed his brow, and extended both hands, palms upward. The air above them shimmered and coalesced into a globe three feet in diameter. Its cloudy surface cleared to show hundreds of Zvejys cowering on a long pier, surrounded by Alan's Forsworn. Alan strode among the terrified captives, crescent-bladed ax hanging loosely in his right hand. He halted and looked out at the ship anchored in the bay.

Carol saw herself standing at the prow, Arn's black-garbed form standing alongside her. This other Carol gave a slow nod and the muscles bunched in Alan's arms, back, and shoulders. His great ax whirled so fast that it became a blur amidst the fountains of blood and gore that rained upon his face and body. The little people screamed and cried. Some tried to run, others to dive into the bay, but Carol gestured, freezing the wailing victims in place.

The imagery played out over a handful of minutes, so realistic that Carol found herself sickened, despite knowing the scene was a lie created by a warped mind. Arn's rage threatened to pull them out of the vision, but Carol calmed him. She needed to see this through to its end.

At last Alan found no one else to butcher. He stood on the pier, soaked in the blood of the innocents. Then the false Carol gestured again, and the corpses piled along the jetty withered, flesh and blood turning to dust, leaving only bones and scraps of clothing behind.

When the bubble faded away, Kragan slowly lowered his hands.

Queen Afacere's face tightened into a mask of dismay.

"They call that butcher the Chosen," Kragan said. "The witch is his sister. We welcomed these strangers into our village. They gathered the people like sheep at a sacrificial slaughter. The Chosen asked only one question of everyone."

"Which was?"

"Where are Landrel's time stones?"

Queen Afacere's gasp escaped the hand that suddenly covered her lips.

"I escaped by cloaking myself with elemental magic. I have journeyed here to give you this warning. The Chosen seeks the holiest treasure in each of the five cities. I offer my humble services to help you stop him."

—⁓—

The vision dissolved, leaving Arn standing beside Carol, staring into Kim's and Galad's concerned faces.

"How long?" Arn asked.

"What?" Kim said.

"He means," Carol said, "how long were we lost in Arn's vision?"

"Just a few moments. But the look on your face startled me. What made you so angry?"

"We saw Kragan," Carol said. "We know what he looks like now."

"And," Arn said, "he's not in Varjupaik."

"So where is he?" Galad asked.

"I don't know. But we're about to find out."

A Varjupaik courier's arrival interrupted their discussion.

"Prince Galad and Princess Kimber, King Trgovec invites your company into the city. We have arranged boarding facilities for your people."

"Good," Kim said. "Escort them into the city. Prince Galad and I will return to the palace to arrange for a room for my sister and her husband."

"As you wish."

It took almost an hour to settle into the merchant marine barracks left empty by the deployment of the Varjupaik fleet. Although Carol and Arn agreed to King Trgovec's offer of a room adjacent to Kim's within his palace, they first accompanied the Forsworn to see where they were being housed. Alan chose to bunk alongside his warriors.

As Arn studied their surroundings, Carol observed everything through his eyes. Once Carol expressed her satisfaction with the adequacy of her company's accommodations, she walked at Arn's side as he followed the king's messenger to the palace. Arn noted how several of the brightly garbed citizens stopped to stare at his wife, apparently startled by the ease with which she navigated her surroundings despite obvious blindness.

Kim met them at the palace doors.

"Thank you, courier. I will escort my sister and her husband from here."

The man gave a slight bow and departed.

When Kim made no attempt to take Carol's hand, her inaction didn't surprise Arn. She was well aware of her sister's magical abilities.

"I've told King Trgovec of your role in our company," Kim said to Carol. "He wishes to speak with you after you get settled."

"Good," Arn said. "We have questions."

Kim turned her attention to him. Arn recalled the terrified young woman whom he, John, and Ty had rescued from Charna and her vorgish slavers. Experience and tragedy had forged her into the person who now stood before him. She had grown strong in both will and magic, but her once-abundant joy and enthusiasm had retreated somewhere deep inside.

"It would be better if you let Carol ask them. The king has a weakness for the opposite sex."

Two days after negotiating a treaty that would eventually place Kim in Trgovec's court as the Endarian ambassador, she was already behaving like one. That was fine with Arn. Court intrigue had long been one of his specialties.

When he and Carol dropped their bundles within their lushly appointed chamber, Kim escorted them to their audience with Trgovec. New visions repeatedly threatened to sweep him away, but Carol's consciousness was stoutly enmeshed with his, and her will was the strongest Arn had ever known. Add to that her mastery of meditation and mental battles with powerful elementals, and she posed a most formidable anchor to reality.

Perhaps in the weeks to come he would learn to passively sample these dream worlds while operating in the real world, but he was far from having that expertise with his time-sight.

Arn was somewhat surprised when Kim led them into the king's council chambers instead of his throne room. The king was seated at the head of a rectangular table surrounded by thirteen chairs. He was a stout man with wolfish eyes set in a jovial face. Kim failed to bow as Arn and Carol did, the princess intentionally testing the strength of her newfound hold on the ruler. With a raised eyebrow, Trgovec let her action pass unchallenged.

"Please be seated," Trgovec said, indicating seats along the table on his left and right.

Kim seated herself to the king's right, Carol slid onto a chair opposite her sister, and Arn sat down next to her. Trgovec directed his gaze at Carol, concern furrowing his brow.

"I am deeply sorrowed by your injury. Should I lay hands on the perpetrator, I vow to serve harsh judgment."

Arn found Carol's smile glorious to behold, her pale eyes serving only to emphasize her expression.

"Thank you, Majesty. Should my desire come to fruition, that will not prove necessary."

"Princess Kimber tells me that you have questions for me."

"As I recovered from the attack upon me, I received a vision of a tiny man with shoulder-length tan hair."

"One of the Zvejys people like those you found massacred in the fishing village of Klampyne."

"He was in a queen's throne room. He called her Afacere."

Trgovec's eyes widened and he sucked in a sharp breath.

"Afacere is the queen of the port city of Jogi. Her brother, Troc, is king of Vurtsid, another of the five seaport city-states on Sadamad. I cannot believe that she would consort with a mass murderer of his own people."

"Kragan is a master deceiver and wielder of both life and mind magics. I sense that the visions he portrayed to Afacere pervert the truth, masking his actions while placing the blame on us."

When the king hesitated, Kim spoke.

"I have explained the mission my mother assigned us. We must visit the other merchant kings and queens of Sadamad to seek additional trading alliances. I need a map of Sadamad."

"And you shall have one. But venture not to Rukkumine. King Godus spawned a treacherous attack on Varjupaik, murdered Queen

Lielisks, severely damaged our temple, and stole our most prized artifact. He started the war that I will end with his death."

Arn felt Carol's trepidation even as his own heart jumped at this revelation. Someone had stolen one of Landrel's time stones, within which he'd secured one of his artifacts of magic amplification. Arn didn't believe that King Godus was the culprit.

One name came to mind, of course. Kragan. And in stealing that artifact, their enemy had acquired the fearsome new magic that almost killed Carol.

9

Southern Kalnai Mountains
YOR 415, Late Summer

It took two weeks for General Bojevnik, King Trgovec's local commander, to gather the wagons, stock them with supplies, and assign the hundred soldiers who would escort the Endarian royals and their company into the Kalnai Mountains. By the time they finally exited the city, Carol was beside herself with impatience. She'd spent much of that time working with Arn to help him learn to control his time-sight.

Those sessions had threatened to pull her husband from the now into vivid alternate futures. She'd felt Arn's desperation at his inability to distinguish what was truly happening from the events that might come to pass. Carol's tether back to her own body served as his safety line from the dream world, pulling Arn from the hallucinations that each practice session unleashed.

But Carol couldn't keep a constant connection to Arn's mind. He deserved privacy. And when he left her side, she lost awareness of her immediate surroundings. Although she could establish the link with anyone she touched, the only other people who felt comfortable with her mind invasions were Kim and Alan.

King Trgovec occupied an exceptional amount of Kim's time discussing all manner of trade between Varjupaik and Endar. She and Galad attended numerous meetings with the wealthiest merchants in the city, going over old maritime maps. They highlighted the routes that would carry ships to the rift that Galad had torn through the time-mists surrounding the Endarian Continent.

When she was alone, Carol lost herself in meditation. She could still summon elementals to cast spells, but without the ability to see, she couldn't choose a target for the magic. Carol even tried seeing through the eyes of elementals, but their sight was confined to the planes where they existed, a view so incomprehensible that it left her unbalanced and nauseous.

A week into their stay in Varjupaik, Kim delivered a solution. The cat was tiny for an adult, weighing no more than two fist-size stones. Carol first saw the animal when Kim placed a hand on Carol's arm, enabling her to form their bond. The cat's long hair was a silky black, and when Carol stroked it, she could feel and hear the feline purr.

"What is its name?" she asked.

"He doesn't yet have one."

"Does he have an owner?"

"If you want him."

Carol took the cat from Kim, pleased that it rested limply in her arms.

"I will call him Leles, after the cloth doll my father gave me when I was a little girl."

She shifted her bond from Kim to Leles, touching the animal's mind as gently and lovingly as possible so as not to startle him. He didn't stiffen or try to pull away from her as she absorbed his senses. Carol passed him a mental picture accompanied by desire, and Leles jumped up onto her left shoulder and looked at Kim.

Her sister smiled, and Carol mirrored her expression.

"He's wonderful," Carol said. "Thank you for finding him for me."

"You need a constant companion. No matter how much your family loves you, we can't be that."

Now, as Carol walked beside Arn with Leles resting on her left shoulder, she savored the memory. She'd bonded with the cat the moment she first held him. Leles granted her the freedom to move about on her own. More importantly, he helped her to exercise her magic. The cat's night vision, sense of smell, and hearing made for a heady mix of enhanced sensations.

The small animal preferred to rest on her shoulder whenever she was awake. Occasionally Carol shifted her mental link to Arn to allow Leles to nap, but the cat seemed perfectly happy to match his sleep cycle to hers.

Carol looked at Arn. Dressed in the black Endarian garb that Queen Elan had given him, he moved as silently as a shadow. He had carved a new haft for Slaken from the tusk of a sea mammal that the Varjupaik soldiers called a mroz. The white handle seemed oddly out of place attached to the ebony blade that Arn wore at his side.

Arn's brow furrowed in an expression of concentration that Carol recognized. He was anchoring himself in the real world while under assault from another of the visions that his time-sight triggered. Carol stifled an impulse to shift her link from her cat to her husband so that she could bolster his concentration. Arn needed to strengthen his ability to control the waking dreams that distracted him. That came only through practice.

The mists formed around the company, masking the world where time moved more slowly. Galad had spent the last several days getting the Varjupaik soldiers under his command accustomed to moving in and out of the time-mists he channeled. Although the regiment had gotten better at such maneuvers, Carol could sense their nervousness. This would be the first time the soldiers would travel a significant distance within a rychly zone.

Leles seemed unfazed by their transition into a zone where days would pass while only a few hours went by in the normal world. As was Galad's practice when traversing lands where enemies might abound, he periodically cleared the mists to regain his bearings and study the countryside that lay ahead.

At each of these stops, Carol summoned an air elemental to lens the air, making quite distant objects appear close at hand. As they passed from the foothills into the southern Kalnai Mountains, she was the first to spot the clansmen.

As she prepared for another trip through the mists, Arn stumbled over a rock and almost fell. He pressed both hands to his face and sat down hard.

"What is it?" Carol asked, kneeling by his side.

When he didn't respond, she shifted her bond from Leles to her husband. And as she did so, the world faded away around her.

—⚬—

The wind howled into a narrow canyon as if it intended to rip down the trees that clung to the rocky slopes. Although Arn couldn't feel the gusts in this ethereal form, he heard it. Low down on the opposite ridge, hundreds of armored soldiers fought beneath an unfamiliar standard. The battle flag sported a hooked spear at the end of a coiled rope, all set against a deep-blue background.

A tight group of Kalnai clansmen was backed up against a cliff face, struggling desperately to keep from being overrun. Their knee-length leather and chain armor were drenched in blood, but Arn couldn't tell how much of it came from the bodies piled up before them and how much from their own wounds. There was no escape. All the horn-helmeted mountain warriors were going to die. And Arn had the sense that someone vital to Alan's future was among them.

—⚬—

Heading into a stiff breeze, Alan strode at the head of his twoscore Forsworn, his lover and two good friends matching his stride. Kat walked at his right hand, with Bill Harrison and Quincy Long two steps behind. The one hundred soldiers that King Trgovec had placed under Galad's command followed alongside the supply wagons. Alan couldn't judge the quality of the swarthy soldiers from Varjupaik, but they were well disciplined, and their company commander exercised tight control over his lieutenants, two promising signs. Still, this was hardly the battle-hardened fighting company that he'd led from Endar Pass.

"Quincy," Alan said, "what do you make of our new recruits?"

"I'll let you know after I've seen them fight."

"Considering the hill people who've been scouting us," Bill said, "you might not have long to wait."

"They might come down to say hello," Kat said.

"That would be nice," Quincy said.

"We should gather some flowers," Bill said.

"Kat, why don't you go cut some," Quincy said. "A woman's touch is needed."

"I might cut something," she said. "I doubt that you'll enjoy it."

Alan led his three friends up onto a rocky outcropping, signaling for the rest of the troops to continue their march. He raised his far-glass to scan the opposite ridgeline. As they made their way northeast from Varjupaik, through the Kalnai foothills and up into the Kalnai Mountains, the terrain was growing more rugged.

Now, as he studied the mountains ahead, he saw no sign of the clansmen Carol had reported. But they were probably hiding within the forests that partially draped these heights. He lowered the glass, took a deep breath of the cool, pine-scented air, and stepped out to assume the lead position once more.

If the Kalnai clans wanted trouble, Alan would be happy to deliver it.

—⁓—

Tudor, son of Vahltehr, led a hundred clansmen through a rift from which he would launch his raid upon the company of soldiers who wore the colors of Rukkumine. Today, he would teach King Godus the fallacy of launching an armed incursion into clan territory.

He wore the traditional combat garb of the Kalnai, rough-bottomed boots of thick leather, knee-length pants, and a goat-hide shirt beneath chain mail. Curling ram horns adorned his padded leather helmet. In his right hand rested his tempered-steel battle hammer, spiked at both ends.

He signaled a halt, a silent command that was passed back through the columns of clan warriors. His next command called for hitrosti, one of the druidic potions every clansman in this company carried. Tudor and his hundred downed the dosage in single gulps.

They all knew what came next. Zdravje.

As he swallowed the hitrosti elixir, the first of the three different potions he carried, Tudor felt it take effect. His muscles tingled with fire. Tudor wanted to hurl himself into battle. He gulped down the second elixir. His skin thickened, taking on the texture of stout but supple leather. But Tudor valued the regenerative properties of the draft far more than its protective shielding. Carobno, the last tincture that he and his fellows drained, left a sour taste in his mouth but produced no other physical sensations. For a limited time, it would provide resistance to all but the most powerful magics.

Tudor raised his hammer high above his head, screamed the warbling clan war cry, and charged.

They poured down the ridge, striking into the flank of the Rukkumine formation as the soldiers turned to meet them. Clouds boiled into the sky as the enemy's priest prepared a magical attack. Lightning lanced down from above to hit Tudor and a half dozen of the clansmen who were closest to him.

It felt as if he'd just rolled in cactus, but the carobno potion made their skins into conductors, funneling the energy directly into the ground. But Tudor knew that the attack had also consumed part of the potion's protective effect. That was fine with him. He and his men were already on top of the enemy forces.

His war hammer whined through the air, splitting the shield of his nearest foe to cave in the man's chest. In seconds his hundred were thoroughly intermingled with the Rukkumine force, their blood on fire with hitrosti-fueled rage. Tudor took a long cut down his left forearm but felt no pain. And as he killed the man who'd inflicted it, the wound knitted itself back together, consuming a bit of the zdravje in his system.

Such was the ferocity of their attack that the Rukkumine formation disintegrated. The soldiers broke into panicked flight back down the canyon with Tudor and his warriors in pursuit. He crashed through thick underbrush, leaping over fallen trees, his lungs working hard to provide the oxygen his raging muscles needed. And with each blow he maimed and killed.

The first sign of trouble came when Tudor broke out of the woods into a large clearing only to be met by the charge of a much larger force. The knowledge that he had just led his warriors into the jaws of a trap only served to stoke the firestorm in his veins.

Magical attacks speared into the rushing clansmen from several locations, some of them burning through the protective doses to fell Tudor's fighters. But he and the rest of his warriors raced across the gap to hurl themselves into their enemies.

If they were to die here today, they would make themselves legends.

—⁂—

Carol snapped back into the present as Arn's vision ended. She shifted her mental connection to Leles as she struggled to regain her bearings.

"We need to save those clansmen," Arn said, his voice filled with urgency.

"I felt it too. Someone important is among them."

"I know where we need to be."

"Go to Galad. I'll tell Alan we'll be changing course."

Arn whirled away, his long strides carrying him rapidly along the line of soldiers toward the Endarian prince. Carol spotted Alan at the front of his Forsworn and forged her mind link with her brother.

"Alan. We have a problem."

"What is it?"

"Arn suffered one of his visions. A group of clan warriors is about to be massacred in a canyon not far from here. For some reason I don't understand, they're important to us. Arn has gone to inform Galad to wield the time-mists that will take us there."

"I will send runners to let the Varjupaik troops know that we'll be launching an attack of our own."

Once again, Carol let the cat be her eyes. As word of the change of mission spread through the company, the mists roiled around them. And as Galad extended it, the fogs blocked out the surrounding countryside except for a narrow channel that extended over the steep ridge to their west. Alan led his Forsworn into that corridor at a quick march. There was no need to run. Although it would take several hours to travel to the canyon that was their destination, only a few minutes would pass outside the arcane haze.

Through Leles's nose she sniffed the air while she listened with his feline ears. The odor of sweating bodies accompanied the sound of elevated heartbeats. This march to battle affected her in much the same way. A blue orb of electrical energy crackled to life within her cupped right hand. Since she would soon be forced to deal a fresh dose of deathly magic, Carol practiced wielding her magic through her cat's eyes as she hiked these rugged slopes.

And as she plucked elementals from the planes of fire, air, earth, and water, producing flickering lights, dancing breezes, crawling rocks, and passing showers, a new determination drove out the self-pity that had filled her at the loss of her sight. She resolved to destroy the wielder who threatened the good people of this world.

PART II

The thumb and index fingers of the three ancient masters of time, life, and mind amplify the two most common branches from each type of magic. But the longest fingers augment the third and most powerful offshoots. Thus have I scattered these game pieces across the board.

—From the *Scroll of Landrel*

10

Kragan emerged from the time-mists he wielded through one of the ancient fingers that hung from a necklace beneath his shirt. Spread out before him lay the beautiful port city of Jogi. Unlike the other four merchant kingdoms on Sadamad, Jogi had no protective walls surrounding it. It was home to the largest of the priestly universities on the continent, and its sequence of merchant kings and queens relied upon the mystic might of their many wielders to keep the metropolis secure.

Cloaking himself in invisibility, Kragan walked the cliff-lined coast, basking in the gentle caress of the sea breeze, tasting the salt on his tongue. This bay opened out to the east. Dozens of merchant ships and hundreds of smaller boats painted a colorful tableau upon the waters.

Kragan walked into the city along one of the main thoroughfares, deftly avoiding collisions with the throngs of people who scurried between the various shops and markets. He knew his destination, the University of Dieve. More specifically, the Temple of the Sea Goddess at its center. With each step his anticipation grew. The time stone that formed the cornerstone of the altar would be discolored, an indication that it would soon dissipate, revealing the artifact hidden within.

The university consisted of one huge building built around an expansive central square. An arched entry at the center of each side allowed visitors to pass from the streets beyond into the park that surrounded the aquamarine temple. The priests who studied within the university outnumbered the worshippers, some meditating in the park while others chanted musical prayers to the goddess.

Kragan liked it here. A pity that his visit would be so short-lived. He could sense the magic that was concentrated within this place, a coruscating ripple from the elemental planes. He suffered the temptation to snatch control of an elemental that one of the nearby priests currently commanded, as he had once done with Carol Rafel. But this was not the time to make neophytes aware of his might.

Instead he made his way through the towering temple doors and into the chamber of Dieve. A half dozen turquoise-robed priests knelt in prayer around the rectangular altar that one of Landrel's offspring had built of time stones. Dozens of other worshippers wandered slowly around the great room, staring at the murals honoring the sea goddess or with heads bowed in contemplation.

None of the wielders of priestly magic sensed his presence as he moved silently among them. He approached the altar, feeling a lump forming deep in his throat. One of the kneeling priests blocked his view of the cornerstone, so Kragan moved to a position where he attained an oblique view of his target. Kragan balled his hands into fists to quell the tremors that passed through them. Something was wrong.

The cornerstone was the same brilliant shade of white as the other time stones from which the dais was constructed. Kragan suppressed the overwhelming urge to hurl the priest who partially blocked his vision aside. Instead he lensed the air to enable himself to more closely study the block.

Impossible. There was no sign of impending dissolution to release the token it contained.

With a thousand questions whirling through his head, Kragan slipped from the temple. He needed to be somewhere quiet and secure so he could study the copy he'd made of the *Scroll of Landrel*. Surely it would reveal some clue that he'd missed.

He hurried down the main avenue and exited onto a narrow alley that exuded a smell indicative of a privy bucket collection route, not surprised that he was the only person to traverse this path. After fifty paces Kragan came to a stop and released his hold on the elemental who concealed him, becoming visible again.

Kragan plucked the earth elemental Urvas from its plane of existence. A hole in the ground opened before him, complete with stone steps leading down. Kragan walked into that shadowed space as the entrance filled in above him.

—ɯ—

For six hours Kragan pored over the portion of the scroll he'd believed he understood. He almost missed the critical clue that unraveled another of Landrel's frustrating ciphers. Unlike the other puzzles Kragan had solved within the text, this cipher wound its way through the document from rear to front. Only when he reversed the order of the words did he understand their meaning.

The meaning of this new text stunned him and completely changed his strategy. He'd intended to steal the cornerstones just before each one was to reach the end of its planned existence, gaining power as he acquired each artifact. But this new cipher caused him to change course. The last three altar cornerstones wouldn't dissolve until they were placed together so that each stone touched both of its sisters.

So he would gain no advantage in collecting them one by one. But there was a way he could influence the merchant kings and queens of

Jogi, Vurtsid, and Paradiis to gather their holy altar cornerstones in one place while also drawing out Carol Rafel. The northernmost city-state of Paradiis became the center of his plan.

Kragan reemerged from the cavern he'd created, climbing stone steps into the dusky alley above. A cry of astonishment caused him to turn. A shoddily dressed man backed slowly away from Kragan, still holding the bucket he'd just emptied into the back of the honey-wagon. He dropped the bucket and spun away. Before he could take a step, Kragan bound him in glowing red bands that stifled his attempted scream.

The bands lifted the fellow into the air and deposited him into the cave Kragan had just climbed from. Then, with a dismissive wave of his hand, Kragan closed the stone passage, entombing the unfortunate soul and returning the alley to its original state.

He walked away, ignoring the horse and foul wagon. This time Kragan didn't bother to make himself invisible. Instead he retraced his steps to the university courtyard and the temple at its center, disregarding the curious stares of people who had never seen a Zvejys. At one time the amused looks would have shamed him to his core. Now they were beneath his notice.

As he approached the massive temple doors, he assumed an exhausted and desperate air and spoke to a priestess at the entrance.

"Please, good cleric. I have traveled for many days carrying a distressing message of warning for your high priestess."

The woman's eyes widened as she looked down at him.

"It has been years since I've seen one of the Zvejys people. Small one, you are a long way from home."

"My people are gone. My home is no more."

"What's happened?"

"This message is for your high priestess's eyes and ears. Please take me to the holy one."

The woman pursed her lips and paused before responding.

"Remain here. I will speak to the master of our order to see if Svaty will see you."

"Thank you."

Kragan waited patiently as twilight deepened into nightfall.

The female priest appeared around the left side of the temple, and Kragan turned to meet her.

"High Priestess Svaty will see you in her private chambers in the university. Follow me."

She moved with a long stride that paid no deference to Kragan's stature, forcing him to trot along to keep up. They entered the west wing of the university through a plain-looking wood door, its handle and latch stained from the oils of many hands over the centuries.

Kragan followed her down a long hall, then into a stairwell, where they climbed three levels. A much shorter hallway brought them to another simple door, where the priestess gave three sharp knocks.

"Enter."

She opened the door, ushered Kragan inside, and then stepped out, closing the portal behind her.

Kragan bowed his head respectfully to the woman in the blue robe who was seated in a cushioned armchair.

"Holy One," he said, "thank you for seeing me."

"Please be seated," Svaty said, indicating a similar chair to her right.

"I think it best that I stand for what I have to show you. It wrings my heart to recall the horrors I've borne witness to."

"What have you to show me?"

"My name is Kragan. I was the wielder tasked with protecting Klampyne, the last of the Zvejys fishing villages. I failed at my task. But I carry the memory of the invaders who've entered these lands seeking the time stones secreted in the altars of each of Dieve's five temples. Behold."

Kragan spread his hands, and a shimmering translucent globe formed above them, quickly clearing. The high priestess watched as a strange ship sailed into the harbor to disgorge scores of marauders onto the shore. Svaty's face blanched in the lamplight as she observed the subsequent interrogation and slaughter of Zvejys men, women, and children.

"They call their butcher the Chosen. The witch is his sister."

Svaty leaned back in her chair, the knuckles of her clenched fists white.

"Why did you not bring word of this to Varjupaik or Rukkumine? They're much closer to your home."

"I journeyed to both but arrived too late to give warning. The raiders had already stolen the holy relics from the two temples. The cities are at war, blaming each other for the thefts. Neither Queen Lielisks nor King Godus would see me. That is why, upon my arrival here, I approached you instead of asking for a royal audience."

The high priestess stood.

"Kragan, you show both courage and wisdom. Come with me. I will escort you to Queen Afacere, and you will show her what I've just watched."

Kragan followed Svaty back down the stairs and into a large room where she gave orders to an acolyte to have a driver bring her carriage around. When he climbed in to sit across from her, the high priestess summoned a globe of soft light that floated just above her palm. Her face still held the hard lines that her outrage had placed there.

"Rest assured. My queen will not allow the unworthy invaders to perpetrate their evil here. She will hunt this Chosen and destroy him and his followers."

"If so, the wandering spirits of my people shall find peace indeed."

11

Southern Kalnai Mountains
YOR 415, Late Summer

Alan emerged from the time-mists on a steep ridge as Kat, Bill, Quincy, and the rest of the Forsworn crossed back into the light of day. The wind that howled through the canyon wasn't loud enough to mask the clash of metal, the yells of battle fury, or the shrieks of the wounded and dying on the battlefield below. A few dozen clansmen were pinned against a cliff, where they waged a desperate fight against hundreds of soldiers.

Carol and Arn emerged from the fog with Galad, the hundred Varjupaik troops, and the supply wagons.

"Rukkumine scum," the Varjupaik commander said, pointing at the uniformed soldiers who fought the clansmen.

"Keep their wielders off our backs," Alan told Carol.

Before she could respond, he charged down the slope at the head of his Forsworn. The Varjupaik soldiers would have to keep up. His churning stride carried him into thick woods that clutched at Alan but failed to slow him.

The forest opened to reveal the wide clearing where opposing forces battled. Alan hit the rear of the lines of soldiers, cutting down a half dozen men before they could turn to meet him. With his shield slung across his back, he whirled his ax in a two-handed grip that put all his strength into each blow.

Confusion swept through the enemy ranks as the officers struggled to mount a counterattack. But such was the fury of the Forsworn that those who stood before them tried to retreat into the soldiers trying to press forward to meet the assault. Fireballs arced toward the Forsworn and the soldiers of Varjupaik, only to be deflected into the Rukkumine ranks.

A spear suddenly thrust through a narrow gap between two of the enemy shields to pierce Alan's shoulder, just before his ax split the shaft. He ignored the white-hot pain, pressing the momentum of his attack, the Forsworn forming a wedge with Alan at its point as the Varjupaik soldiers fell upon the enemies who tried to flank his warriors.

"To the clansmen," Alan yelled as his ax split the shield of the soldier in front of him and embedded itself in the fellow's sternum.

He kicked the dying man off his blade and pressed forward. The masses of soldiers who were jammed up in front of Alan struggled to escape.

—∞—

Standing on high ground that sloped up to the cliffs behind him, Tudor bled from a dozen wounds. He fought on. The potion that sped his healing had burned its way through his system, losing potency until it was now gone. Fewer than twoscore of his warriors were still on their feet. But the violence with which they fought and slew the enemies before them filled Tudor with pride.

"Tudor, look!" A clansman on his right yelled and pointed.

The attacking soldiers faltered, confusion sweeping through their ranks. Several turned to look behind them, only to be cut down by Tudor's fighters. For some reason, Rukkumine's priestly wielders of magic were sending fireballs at something behind their troops. He parried a sword with such force that his hammer snapped the blade from its haft. Tudor swung the spiked hammer into the man's head, raining gore on those behind the dead soldier.

More of the enemy turned to meet a new threat that Tudor now saw. Dozens of bald fighters had split their way through the Rukkumine ranks. And at their front, a thickly muscled man whirled an ax with such force that it split armor and severed limbs with every strike.

A thrill shot through Tudor's body, raising the gooseflesh on his arms and legs. This was the moment.

"With me," he yelled, and he charged into the mass of enemies that separated the clansmen from these unknown allies.

The battle cries of his warriors accompanied the tune his hammer sang on the wind.

—◊—

Arn knew that he was standing beside Carol, but he couldn't see or hear her. His mind reeled from one future to another, some close at hand, some distant. In many of these he died, Carol died, Alan died, and Kragan emerged victorious, the nine fragments of Landrel's shattered trident in his possession. Few timelines provided hope.

He sensed a thread of causality that he couldn't follow back to its source. Seemingly insignificant actions where different timelines intersected spawned wildly different outcomes. His head spun.

Arn needed to find his way back to the present. Somehow his mind link with Carol allowed her to pull him from the madness, but she was currently shielding Alan's and Galad's forces from the magical attacks of the Rukkumine priests in the canyon. He had no tether to her.

An emotion he'd never before experienced engulfed him. Arn felt useless. He had become a seer, not a doer. He couldn't fight. He couldn't protect his wife. Right now, in the real world, people Arn cared about were dying in battle while he stood frozen.

His hand tightened around Slaken's haft as if squeezing the ivory handle would give him an anchor. But Slaken's magic was gone. And Arn was a mere babe in this new, deadly wasteland.

—ᗰ—

Magic from the planes of air, fire, and water clawed toward Carol from all sides. For a sickening moment, her shielding faltered before the coordinated attacks that her talented priestly opponents unleashed. Lightning crawled across the invisible surface that protected her, standing Leles's hair on end and pulling an angry hiss from the cat's mouth.

She bit her lip, tasted blood, and strengthened her defenses, deflecting bolts and fireballs into enemy soldiers. Wind howled through the canyon, picking up sticks and gravel, hurling them at the warriors locked in mortal combat. So intense was Carol's concentration that she failed to notice the earth elemental under the rock upon which she stood. The ground gave way beneath her feet, dropping her and Leles into a pit filled with jagged stone spikes.

Carol whipsawed her focus, lashing Betep to her will and arresting her fall two feet above the deadly points. As the air elemental lifted her ten feet above the ground, Carol wrested control of the earth elemental Urvas from its priestly master. The man struggled to eject her mind from Urvas. He failed.

But as she intertwined her thoughts with his, she came to know the wielder named Vludnost. Unlike many of Kragan's followers and allies, this was a good man, devoted to his goddess and the people of Rukkumine. He hadn't been in favor of the war between his city and Varjupaik, but he was here to do his duty. A further realization shook her resolve. Carol was quite sure that the same could be said for many of the soldiers fighting and dying on the battlefield.

"If you promise to cease your magical attacks on me and my people," Carol projected, *"I will spare your life."*

"I will not betray my people and my calling. Do what you must."

Just as she had done with the foul High Protector, she shredded the priest's mind.

The curse of war. Good people found themselves killing each other.

Leles's eyes found Arn, standing erect, eyes unfocused, his hand resting upon Slaken's white haft. With a dull ache in her breast, Carol lowered herself to the ground. She reached out to touch him, but cheers from the clearing below caused her to redirect Leles's gaze.

With the death of their priests, the surviving Rukkumine soldiers were fleeing into the forest. The Varjupaik troops started to pursue them, but Galad ordered them to halt. It was they who raised the victory chorus.

Carol turned back to her husband. She didn't doubt that she could pull him from his trance. Still she hesitated.

No.

She would allow him the opportunity to find his own way back.

—⚶—

Kim made her way among the wounded, exchanging her health for their injuries as she channeled life energy from the dense undergrowth to heal herself. Transferring life from plants was so much slower than exchanging the health of living creatures. Channeling this weaker form of life energy left her empty, devoid of the sensual urges that necrotic magic aroused. If only the Forsworn or the clansmen had taken prisoners, she could have mended these soldiers as she fed her craving on their enemies.

Of the twenty-two Forsworn who had survived, none were unscathed. The same was true for the thirteen clansmen. The Varjupaik soldiers had taken far fewer casualties.

A broken spear jutted through Alan's shoulder, just beneath his collarbone, but he had ordered Kim to tend to the others first. Likewise, the leader of the clansmen deferred to his warriors. When she finally got to Alan, she was glad to see that he had left the shaft in place, plugging the hole it had punched through his body.

Looking at the weapon that had impaled Alan left her queasy, although she had just treated far worse injuries. This wound reminded her of the fatal injury that had stolen John from her. A little lower and the result would have been the same.

Someone had cut away the leather and chain mail from Alan's chest. Now he sat leaning back against a pine tree. She knelt beside him, gently running her fingers around the entry and exit wounds.

"We're going to have to cut the shaft close to your chest and pull it out through your back," she said.

"I'll do it," Katrin said, drawing Kim's gaze to the lean woman.

"We should probably have Bill or Quincy pull it out."

"I said I'll do it."

Seeing Alan's nod, Kim stepped back, preparing herself to channel the healing as soon as Katrin removed the spear.

The Forsworn woman knelt beside Alan and pressed the palm of her left hand flat against his breast, anchoring the shaft that protruded between her index finger and thumb. Then she sawed off the end with her long knife until only an inch remained. Alan's clenched jaw and the beads of sweat on his forehead testified to his pain.

Katrin moved behind Alan. In one swift movement, she grabbed the shaft and yanked it free, pulling a ragged gasp from his lips. She tossed the spear-tip aside and pressed her palms against the chest and back wounds.

As Kim funneled the painful injury into her own body, Alan's wound knitted itself closed. Although she channeled life from the dense undergrowth, it took a few moments longer for her wounded shoulder to heal than it took to mend Alan. Weak with exhaustion and pain, she turned on Katrin.

"Next time give me warning."

"You're the one who owes me a warning. I've seen the way you watch the Chosen when you think he's not looking. I see it in your face even now."

Kim felt the dagger of Katrin's tongue drain the blood from her face.

Alan stood up between them, his balance unsteady.

"Stop it. Both of you. We're all on the same side."

Katrin stalked away without so much as a glance at him. Kim watched her disappear into the woods with grim satisfaction. Alan placed a hand on her shoulder, sending a thrill through Kim that washed away any remaining twinges of pain.

"Thank you," he said, "for what you've done for my Forsworn and the others today. I know how you suffer."

"I do not . . . It goes away."

"Does it? For either of us?"

Tears suddenly filled her eyes. Alan dabbed them away with his thumbs. Since John's death, no man had touched her with such care. Blinking, she stepped back.

"I should check on the others."

"I suppose so."

Then she turned and walked away, feeling his eyes follow her out onto the day's bloody battleground.

—⁓—

As Tudor supervised the collection of his dead, he saw the man who had led the attack on the Rukkumine soldiers walking toward him. The leader of the clansmen turned to meet the impressive warrior with an outstretched hand. When they briefly clasped forearms, Tudor felt as if he grasped tempered steel.

"I am Tudor, son of Clan Chief Vahltehr. One of your warriors told me that your people name you the Chosen."

"That is what they call me."

"You have my deepest gratitude."

"We both lost many brave fighters today."

"One cannot ask more than to die well."

"Except for a life well lived."

"I grant you that. What brings you into our mountains?"

"We pursue a murderer and wielder of magic. We believe he has taken refuge in the port city of Jogi."

"You should have taken a ship."

"Varjupaik and Rukkumine wage war against each other. Sea passage was not possible."

"You will need each chief's permission to pass through their lands."

"And how can I secure that?"

"Allow me to introduce you to my father. He holds some sway with many of the other chiefs."

"But not all?"

"We all have our rivals."

"How far is it back to your clan?"

"Rodina is only a day's march if you can help us bear our dead home."

"We honor our own fallen by burning their bodies. We will do so tonight. Tomorrow we will accompany you home."

"Agreed."

Tudor watched the man with the crescent-bladed ax strapped to his back return to his people, who worked to clear the corpses from the killing field. His thoughts turned to the tall, bald swordsman who had told him the legend of the Chosen.

Having watched this bear of a warrior fight, Tudor could almost believe.

—ᴡ—

Lost in a series of waking dreams, Arn let anger have him. His frustration, born of loss of control, pushed him forward, calling the name of his tormentor.

"Landrel."

As if he had just spoken the word of ages, the dreamscape of death and destruction that surrounded him melted away. Once more he stood on Endar's northeastern plains as a stiff breeze pelted his face with freezing rain. He faced the Endarian time-master. Arn resisted the temptation to plunge his knife into the taller man's chest. There were things he needed to learn from the wielder.

"Why do you fight so hard against that which comes to you naturally?" Landrel asked.

"What game are you playing with us? What are you trying to make me do?"

"As I told you, my time-sight fogs where you're concerned. I cannot make you do anything."

"I don't believe you. You caused a shard of your trident to be hidden within the bone that King Rodan's wielder used to create Slaken's haft. You caused Carol's blinding."

"You taste the lie that just formed on your lips. I showed you how to destroy Slaken, but your reluctance to perform the deed prevented you from seeing the path that could have protected your wife."

The words ripped at Arn, confirming what he already knew.

"But," Landrel said, "the talent to save her from far worse lies within you. Embrace it."

"I'm trying."

"You are not. You were a lost youth when High Lord Rafel saved you from the gallows and turned you over to Gaar to forge you into the weapon you became. The battle master beat you down day after day. You got back up every time. I suggest that you apply that determination to learning to wield your time-sight."

"You will not guide me?"

"Only you can do that. Follow your intuition and learn to protect those you love."

The vision faded into the battle scene that he'd previously departed. Arn forced himself to study the details of his surroundings. He gradually realized he didn't exist in just one dream at a time. The hallucinations overlapped. He could step from one into another by focusing his attention on the latest vision. The images were blurry, but some were sharper than others.

Arn sought clarity. Often the differences were subtle, but he began to acquire an intuitive feel for each move that yielded lucidity.

As a boy he had developed a love of climbing, whether trees, buildings, or towering cliffs. In the beginning he climbed slowly and carefully. But as his technique and confidence improved, he grew to recognize the hand- and footholds that would speed his ascent or descent.

As he moved through dreamscapes, the clues gradually began to make sense. The farther into the future Arn peered, the less distinct the visions that branched out before him became, indicating their likelihood of coming to pass. And depending on what Arn did in one dreamscape, certain paths clarified while others grew hazy.

He moved faster, following a trail through visions that grew ever sharper. When he saw himself cut Charna's head from her neck with Slaken, Arn realized he'd regressed into the past.

Going slower, he retraced his movements. He emerged into the light of day, standing on a steep hillside, his hand on Slaken's hilt. Carol sat with her hands in her lap, her white eyes staring sightlessly in his direction. Relief flooded through Arn. Carol climbed to her feet, her black cat perched on her shoulder. Then his wife was in his arms, her soft lips finding his.

"You found your way," she said.

"Thank you for not helping."

"And you learned."

"I'm now a fully qualified novice."

Carol chuckled. "A big improvement from scared and clueless."

Arn released her and turned to look down at the distant clearing, which now lay in shadows cast by the sinking sun. Soldiers moved across the battlefield, collecting bodies and stacking them in two large piles. One would be friendly dead. The other would be enemies. Closer examination revealed an area in front of the cliff against which the clansmen had been trapped where bodies were laid out side by side in four rows.

"How many did we lose?" he asked.

"Almost half of Alan's Forsworn and twenty-eight of the Varjupaik company died."

"And the Rukkumine losses?"

"More than four hundred dead, including all their wielders. The rest fled southeast."

"What of Alan, Kim, and Galad?"

"All alive," Carol said. "Kim saved as many wounded as she could, including several of the clansmen. She suffered the worst of it."

"And the enemy wounded?"

"The Varjupaik soldiers put them to the sword at their commander's orders. Galad didn't object."

"Death is the toll of war."

"Yes."

"What of the clansmen?"

"Alan met with Tudor, the leader of this company. Tomorrow we will march together to meet Tudor's father, Chief Vahltehr. Alan hopes that Vahltehr will grant us safe passage through his lands and, perhaps, arrange for other chiefs to do the same."

Carol placed a hand on his arm, pulling his attention back to her face.

"Did you see anything in your visions that might guide our next actions?"

"They were such a tangled mess that it was all I could do to find my way out. After I've rested, I'll try again."

"It will wait until tomorrow."

Arn looked at the lengthening shadows.

"Let's get down to the clearing before we lose the light."

Carol held out her right hand, and a shining bubble appeared above it.

"I never lose the light."

"And I'm here to make sure no one ever takes it from you."

12

Tudor, with Alan at his side, crested a rise and halted to savor the view that always filled him with joy. Golden meadows dotted the lush green valley that spread out before them, the idyllic scene framed by the snowcapped mountains that surrounded it. Two leagues from where he stood, hundreds of log cabins with red roofs clustered along the near edge of the azure lake that snaked its way northward between forested hillsides.

"Chosen," he said, "behold Rodina. What think you of my mountain home?"

"It's as beautiful a sight as I have ever seen."

The comment sat well with Tudor. Movement in the woods a hundred paces from where they'd come to a halt caused him to lift his arm and point.

"My father approaches."

"I'm surprised we didn't encounter his warriors earlier."

Tudor laughed. "Be assured that our many eyes in the mountains have been watching our approach since we exited the Endarian time-mists several leagues back. If they hadn't recognized me leading the way, the confrontation would have been unpleasant."

Two dozen warriors accompanied the clan chief, while hundreds more came to a halt a hundred paces behind him. Vahltehr's graying blond hair draped his broad shoulders, but his blue eyes showed none of their usual humor. His trimmed beard highlighted the tight line of his lips, which made plain his disapproval. Despite his long familiarity with the gravitas that emanated from Vahltehr, Tudor found the clan chief's challenging demeanor daunting.

"Father."

"Why do you lead scores of outsiders into our homeland? And why do they bear the bodies of so many of our clansmen?"

"If not for these outsiders, Rukkumine invaders would have killed us all."

Vahltehr turned his attention to Alan.

"Is this their leader?"

"This is the one they call the Chosen. He leads the bald group of elite warriors. He and his Forsworn fought their way through ten times their number to rescue us. Together we routed more than four hundred of our enemies."

Vahltehr addressed the foreign warrior.

"Chosen?"

"Some call me that."

"What do the others call you?"

"My given name is Alan."

Vahltehr rubbed his bearded chin, his brow furrowed in thought.

"What brought you into my lands, and why did you come to the aid of my clansmen?"

"Varjupaik is at war with Rukkumine. We saw our enemies slaughtering a much smaller force. I can't stomach that."

"You do not have the look of the Varjupaik soldiers who accompany you."

"My companions and I have signed a treaty with Varjupaik."

Tudor watched as Vahltehr surveyed the outsiders who bore the bodies of Tudor's fallen clansmen.

"You saved my son, and you helped him bear home our honored dead. I find myself in your debt."

Vahltehr stepped forward and gripped arms with the Chosen.

"Welcome to Rodina."

—⁂—

Commander Vrah surveyed the ten thousand soldiers who comprised what remained of Rukkumine's army. He should have had three times that number assembled here, but most of his soldiers had been ordered onto ships to confront the Varjupaik fleet.

And now one of his battalions had just been routed by some Kalnai clansmen, supported by a company of Varjupaik soldiers and a group of bald barbarians. He stepped close enough to get nose-to-nose with the battalion commander responsible for this stain on Vrah's previously unblemished record.

"Take off your shirt and face the regiment. I should lash you myself. But since I want to watch, I leave that to the good sergeant."

Vrah turned to the soldier holding the whip.

"Twenty lashes. Every time he yelps, add another."

"Yes, Commander."

Vrah walked to his place beside his sergeant major. He turned on his heel, his back to his soldiers, facing the spectacle that was about to unfold before them. The whip unfurled, then hissed and cracked. To the former battalion commander's credit, he remained silent until the fifteenth bloody stroke. After that, things went badly.

When the beating finally stopped, the bloody mess that had once been a man lay sprawled facedown in the dirt.

Commander Vrah looked to his right.

"Sergeant Major."

"Sir?"

"Ready the regiment for the march. We're going to clean the clan scum from these mountains."

—⁂—

Arn awoke in darkness, the image of the ruined corpse still so real that the metallic smell of blood clung to his nostrils. He sat up, struggling to recall where he was. Ah yes. Vahltehr had given their company sleeping space inside the longhouse that alternatively served as the clan's meeting center and its dance hall. The scent of pine sap still oozing from the log walls helped drive away the dream.

Arn reached out to place his right hand on the rough surface of the wall beside which he and Carol had spread their bedrolls. Like the hundreds of cabins that clustered near the lake, this much larger structure stood strong enough to bear the weight of heavy winter snow.

The darkness within the building draped his shoulders with the weight of chain mail. The snores of sleeping warriors proclaimed a battle weariness that Arn shared.

By the dark gods, he longed for the peaceful respite he had shared with Carol within the sanctuary of Misty Hollow. Would they ever again know such tranquility, or were they destined to end their lives in strife? Damn Kragan to the deep pits. And Landrel along with him.

"What is it?" Carol asked. "What's wrong?"

"They're coming."

He felt her sit up beside him, Leles assuming his customary perch on her left shoulder.

"Who?"

"The army of Rukkumine, to massacre the clan for what we did."

Though Arn knew her cat's eyes didn't need it, Carol created just enough light for him to see. Having slept fully clothed, they slipped into their boots. Then they silently made their way through the rows of sleepers stretched out beneath blankets on the wood-plank floor.

At the doorway Carol doused her ethereal flame. Arn stepped out into the moonlit street under the star-filled sky. He took a deep breath.

"The fighting never ends, does it?" Carol asked.

"I don't see it stopping."

"But Landrel does?"

"I think so."

"Do you still believe he's trying to manipulate us?"

"I suspect he's using our war with Kragan to create the result he desires. It might not be an outcome that we like."

"How can we find out what Landrel hopes to achieve?"

"It's time for me to try the artifact I took from Slaken."

"Tonight?"

"I may not be ready, but I'm afraid we can't wait any longer."

Carol wrapped her arms around his neck, hugging him hard, as if she could shield him with her body.

"Okay," Carol said, releasing Arn and summoning a dim light. "Let's find a secluded place for you to make the attempt."

Arn allowed himself to sample the sharpest and nearest of futures, watching as guards came and went, noting their movement patterns. He took Carol's hand and walked out of the town and into the forest. He found a place where they could sit facing each other on a bed of pine needles.

He sat down, legs crossed, and Carol mirrored his posture. Leles leapt down from her shoulder, curled up beside her, and closed his eyes. Arn felt the gentle caress of Carol's thoughts as she linked her mind to his.

Taking the pouch from his belt, Arn loosened its drawstring and dumped its contents onto the ground. He suppressed the urge to crack his knuckles, swallowed, and then picked up the finger.

The dreamscape that exploded in his mind took his breath away. A thousand images fought for his attention as the threads of possible futures roiled, intertwining and diverging. Arn felt his heart beating faster and faster and fought to calm himself. Carol's thoughts penetrated the cacophony.

Think about Landrel. Find the futures he touched most heavily.

Of course she was right. How had he allowed himself to forget his goal?

When nothing changed, Arn shifted to one of the meditation methods that Carol had taught him. He allowed the plethora of images to shrink until they were a mere pinpoint of light in a sea of blackness. He sent a single thought spiraling toward that dot.

Landrel.

It was a command. A summons.

Ever so slowly, tiny strands of brightness spiraled outward from the pinpoint. At first dozens, then hundreds. A daunting number of possibilities. Locking the image of the bright threads into his memory, Arn picked one and slipped into it.

—␣⁓␣—

Arn was sucked into a dreamscape so real that he could feel the heat from the funeral pyre on his face and arms. Flames licked the night sky, sending a shower of sparks floating away on the breeze. Hundreds of people he recognized stood looking at the fire, many openly weeping. One of these hid her face in her hands. But he would know his wife anywhere.

Suddenly the crowd parted to let a bare-chested warrior with a shoulder-length blond mane through. The man held the crescent-bladed ax that had once belonged to Arn's dead friend, Ty. As if he had heard Arn's thoughts, the tall warrior turned his head to meet Arn's gaze. Arn felt as though he had been kicked in the stomach. Ty.

He spoke five words that reached Arn's ears above the roar of the flames.

"Blade. This has to be."

Before Arn had a chance to respond, Ty spread his arms wide, then whirled his ax in a blur before him, making it howl through the air. A ten-foot-wide hole opened in the center of the flames. Without another glance back, Ty strode into the fire-ringed void to grasp the wrist of a man whom Ty's body blocked from Arn's view.

When Arn reached out, as if to pull Ty from the flames, he felt something fall from his open hand. He was snatched from the vision with such force that everything faded to black. The last thing Arn felt was the side of his head striking the tree.

—⚏—

Carol snapped back into herself, her mental link to her husband broken so abruptly that it sent a fiery lance through her brain. A moan escaped her lips. She heard a solid *thunk* from the spot where Arn had been sitting.

"Leles," she said, relieved to feel the cat crawl into her arms.

But when Carol tried to connect her mind with that of Leles, she failed. The pounding in her head grew so intense that she had to fight back nausea. Carol released Leles, rolled to her knees, and felt her way forward.

"Arn?"

Nothing.

Then her right hand touched his leg. Tracing her way up his body, she found that he was lying on his right side.

"Arn?"

Her hand touched his cheek, feeling sticky wetness. Her heart thumped. His hair was matted with warm blood oozing from a cut high on the left side of his head.

Carol's hands found the tree, and she pulled herself to her feet, clinging to the trunk as wave after wave of dizziness tried to fell her. She took a deep breath and yelled.

"Kim!"

With the strength leaching from her body, Carol repeated her call, over and over, until she felt hands grip her shoulders.

"She is coming," Galad said.

Carol's legs gave out, and only his strong grip kept her from collapsing on top of Arn. He lowered her to the ground, letting her lean back against the pine.

"What happened?" Kim asked.

"Arn hit his head. He's bleeding badly."

Carol heard heavy footsteps as others gathered around them, their agitated queries merely a fading buzz in her ears.

—☉—

Kim knelt beside Carol, her face lit by the torch that Alan held, ignoring him, Galad, and the several clansmen who had come at Carol's call. Her life magic could detect no sign of injury on her sister's body.

Arn's head injury was serious enough that Kim took her time absorbing his wound. It would do him no good for her to lose consciousness by trying to heal the injury too quickly.

The horror of killing these lovely trees and shrubs sickened her as much as the agony she endured, the act recalling the memory of the wasteland she had left behind in Endar Pass. When she was done, she ran the tips of her fingers over the scalp on the left side of Arn's head. Despite the blood that matted his hair and smeared his face, no trace of the injury remained.

Satisfied that she had done all that she could, she started to get to her feet. Then she saw it, lying on the pine needles beside Arn. The mummified finger that Arn had been afraid to touch. Why had he and Carol brought the artifact out into the woods? Whatever ritual he and Carol had conducted, this foul thing had caused their trauma. Despite her revulsion, Kim slipped her sleeve down over her right hand, picked up the artifact, and returned it to Arn's pouch. That simple action left her shuddering.

With a deep breath, Kim rose to her feet just as a commotion broke out around her. She turned to see a group of women shove their way through the clansmen who'd gathered. The nine ladies wore hooded brown robes with sleeves long enough that only their fingertips showed. The one who struck Kim as the leader reached out to touch a withered strand of what had just been a thriving green vine, her face a mask of fury as it crumbled away at her touch.

She raised her hand to point directly into Kim's face.

"Upir."

Kim had no idea what the word meant, but from the old woman's tone, it sounded like a curse. The others closed in around her, echoing their leader's pronouncement.

"Upir."

Suddenly Alan shoved his way through the cluster to place his body between Kim and the women.

"Back away. Do not make me move you."

Then Galad was there, protecting her other side.

Vahltehr stepped forward. "What's the meaning of this, Saman?"

The old woman turned on the chief.

"This upir is a user of dark magic. She is a life-stealer. Bear witness."

The crone grabbed a handful of shriveled vines and crumbled them before Vahltehr's face.

"Enough," Vahltehr said. "All of you, return to your homes or places of duty. Right now."

For several moments the old woman held Vahltehr's gaze. Then, with a hiss, she turned her back on him and walked away. The other druids followed her into the night. The rest of the crowd dispersed, leaving only Kim, Alan, Galad, and Vahltehr standing over Carol and Arn's unconscious forms.

"We will speak no more of this tonight," Vahltehr said. "Care for your injured."

Then he too departed.

Alan knelt to pick up Carol, and Galad lifted Arn into his arms.

—⧉—

Kragan had accomplished something that no one else would have believed possible. He had so impressed Queen Afacere with his intellect and magical talent that she had ensconced him in her palace, much to the chagrin of her closest advisers. Although she had at first doubted his description of the events in Klampyne and the threat posed by the Chosen, her emissaries had confirmed the theft of the precious relics from the temples in Varjupaik and Rukkumine.

There had also been rumors of barbarians and clansmen led by a brawny warrior and a blind witch defeating a Rukkumine battalion with ten times their number. The descriptions had so closely matched the scenes Kragan had shown her that Afacere's doubts had evaporated. The description of the witch had given Kragan the most pleasure. He had not killed Carol Rafel, but he had left her disfigured and blinded. That alone was worth the sacrifice of Charna.

If his understanding of the ciphers in the *Scroll of Landrel* was correct, the Chosen was already beginning to gather a following that would sweep northward from the Kalnai Mountains to descend on Jogi.

Precisely what he wanted.

—⧉—

Daybreak arrived along with a dense fog that draped the clan township of Rodina. Last night, Kim had healed Arn's wound, but neither the assassin nor Carol had regained consciousness. Carol worried her the most. Kim had still found no sign of physical injury to her sister.

She simply wouldn't wake up, despite Kim's gentle nudges. And the black cat remained on her chest, where he had curled up when Alan had rested Carol on her bedding.

Kim had the odd impression that Carol would awaken only when Arn did. Had her mental link to her husband been so strong that they remained bound together? Perhaps sleep was all they needed.

She stepped out of the longhouse, the dampness of the air chill against her skin. Shadows moved through the street, so indistinct that she couldn't make out if they were clansmen or -women. The memory of the nine druids flooded into her mind. Even here on Sadamad, people despised Kim's use of necrotic magic. And those women had certainly not seen the worst forms of it.

Her mood as dismal as the weather, Kim returned to the longhouse. She would keep watch over Carol and Arn until they recovered.

—ᴍ—

Carol knew that she had opened her eyes even though they revealed nothing more than when they were closed. Leles rubbed his soft face against her neck, as if to say it was about time she awoke. Carol sat up, cradling the cat in her arms. She touched his mind, feeling an intense relief when she formed the connection that enabled her to see.

"You had me petrified," Kim said when Carol looked up at her.

A groan from Carol's right shifted her attention to Arn, who stretched and sat up. He tried to run a hand through his hair but found it caked with dried blood. Suddenly he grabbed for the pouch at his belt, relief smoothing his brow as he felt the contents within.

"I found the dread thing and put it in your pouch," Kim said. "I was careful not to touch it."

"Good."

"How are you two feeling this morning?"

"My headache is gone," Carol said.

"I think you gave it to me," Arn said. "But my skull seems to have knitted itself back together. Thank you for that."

"You're welcome," Kim said.

"Where are the others?" Arn asked.

"Alan and Galad have assembled the soldiers in the village square. They need to reorganize the fighting units after our combat losses."

"They need to know that the Rukkumine army is coming," Carol said.

"So does Vahltehr," Arn said. "But first, I think I'll wash up. Cold water might help ease the throbbing in my skull."

The idea of getting clean appealed to Carol as well.

She and Arn found Vahltehr and Tudor when they returned from the creek. The two were engaged in a heated conversation, and she picked up a few words through the cat's ears as they approached.

"Don't let the druids drive these people away," Tudor said.

"I will talk to them, but if they stop making potions—"

"The crone and her sisters will not hold me hostage to their magic. Theirs is not the only wisdom."

Vahltehr noticed the couple's approach and held up a hand to silence his son.

Both men turned toward them, Tudor struggling to calm himself. The chief smiled.

"So good to see that you've recovered."

"Unfortunately," Carol said, "we bear foul tidings."

"How so?"

"My husband, Arn, has had a vision."

"Is he a seer?"

"Yes."

"I have little faith in fortune-tellers."

"As you should. Arn's gift is different. It was he who led us to rescue your son and his clansmen."

Vahltehr stared hard at Arn.

"So . . . ," he said haltingly, "what is this bad news you wish to deliver?"

"I don't wish to deliver anything. But you need to hear the message."

"Yet you keep me waiting. A common diviner's tactic."

"Several thousand of Rukkumine's soldiers will be heading here to murder your clan and burn your mountain stronghold."

"Why?"

"Your warriors humiliated the army commander by killing hundreds of his soldiers and forcing the rest to flee like cowards."

"Your Chosen did that."

"And your son started the battle."

"I don't believe you."

"You have scouts."

"They have reported no such movement."

"I see the future, not the present. I urge you to send them southeast."

"Chief Vahltehr," Carol said, "I attest that you can rely upon what my husband tells you. I have seen into his mind."

Vahltehr laughed and turned to Tudor.

"You bring me a traveling caravan filled with heroes, diviners, and charlatans."

Carol linked to Vahltehr's consciousness, replicating Arn's vision in every detail, holding up her hand to cut off Tudor's angry response. And as that dream ran its course, a gasp escaped the chieftain's lips. He hefted his war hammer, readying himself to face the vast army that poured into his mountain homeland. Fury rushed in to displace an initial sense of dread.

When she released Vahltehr from the nightmare, Carol spoke a single word.

"Charlatans?"

—⁓—

Alan clasped wrists with Tudor, seeing the flash in his blue eyes. This man was rapidly becoming another true friend. It saddened him. Nine of every ten of Alan's allies died in battle alongside him. Was he or was he not the Chosen, destined to recruit history's greatest warriors, who would perish in battle to rise again to fight alongside the Dread Lord in the land of the dead?

"So what says your father?"

"I think he believes Arn," Tudor said. "I hope so."

"And the druids?"

"They are jealous guardians of their status. They see other magics as unholy and unnatural threats."

"So you would join my Forsworn and become one of my brothers?"

"I have fought alongside you. You battle with a ferocity that is beyond that of any mortal. You are the Chosen, as surely as I live. All my life, one core value has driven me. Honor. I would be a part of your legacy."

"What does Vahltehr think of your choice?"

"I have told my father of my decision. He is not happy, but it is what I desire."

Kat stepped forward and embraced Tudor, giving him a loud smack on the back when she released him.

"You do realize you have to shave your head?" Quincy said.

"Women like my hair."

"Have no fear," Kat said, a smirk on her lips. "They'll still come calling."

Tudor considered this as several moments passed. Then, as he met Katrin's gaze, a broad grin spread across his face.

"If you shave it."

"Sit down," she said, her knife making a whisking sound as she drew the blade from its sheath. "Do you want it done right or quick and bloody?"

Tudor sat down on the ground. "Take your time."

Alan watched the shearing as the rest of his warriors gathered around Tudor.

When the ceremony ended, Tudor stood, his scalp white under the sun that had burned away the morning fog. So skillfully had Kat employed her blade that she'd inflicted no nicks or scratches.

Alan stepped forward and embraced him.

"Welcome to the Forsworn."

13

Rodina, Southern Kalnai Mountains
YOR 415, Late Summer

Arn stood on a ridgeline beside Alan, Carol, and Kim twenty leagues southeast of the clan township of Rodina. Galad had channeled the time-mists that had brought the Forsworn here, along with a thousand of Vahltehr's warriors and dozens of Varjupaik soldiers. The Rukkumine army poured into the cliff-lined valley below them, ten thousand strong, headed toward the narrow pass that would grant them access to Vahltehr's highlands.

Vahltehr and his clan would have to hold that pass. The Forsworn and the Varjupaik soldiers, supported by Carol, Arn, and the Endarian siblings, would form the poisonous viper that struck at their enemy's heels.

For the last several days, Arn had worked himself to exhaustion experimenting with controlling his visions, limiting them to the immediate future in his vicinity.

Just as importantly for him personally, he was learning to fight again, this time while employing his waking dreams. Quincy had been his sparring partner, each of them using sticks instead of sword and knife. For the first several sessions, the lanky swordsman had left Arn covered with black-and-blue bruises that he refused to let Kim heal. Pain locked the lessons into place in Arn's mind and provided an increased sense of urgency.

He could now see what would play out depending on which actions he took. He could replay a scenario dozens of times in rapid sequence until he found the path of greatest advantage. And he had gotten fast enough that this ever-changing foresight no longer slowed his natural reactions.

In the past he had relied on his intuition to cue him to an opponent's attack before it occurred. This new and evolving skill had already surpassed the level he'd previously attained. The downside was how quickly his exertions tired him.

"Looks like the action is about to get started," Alan said, pointing to the lead elements of the Rukkumine forces.

They were making their way into the pass, where the walls of the canyon closed to within three hundred paces of each other. Vahltehr and his clansmen would be waiting to meet them just beyond the first sharp bend, a twist in the terrain that would shelter them from enemy archers and magical attacks from afar. It would also allow Vahltehr to rotate his warriors, sending forward reserves who had just consumed their enhancement potions, replacing the frontline fighters whose mystic tinctures had worn off.

Arn saw turmoil ripple through the enemy several moments before he heard the distant clash echo through this canyon.

"They're bunching up," Alan said.

"Wait for it," Arn said, sampling the vision storm that cycled through the protected corners of his mind.

Carol magnified the distant scene. Just as Arn had foretold, follow-on troops pressed forward toward the battle, jamming the entrance to the pass with bodies. Clouds boiled into the sky above the cliffs as arcane fireballs arced outward from within the massed enemy. These exploded into the cliffs that formed the sharp bend in the canyon, loosing boulders that bounded downward, gathering companions that plummeted onto the Rukkumine soldiers.

"Now?" she said.

"Yes."

"I will stay up here," Carol said, "where I can provide the best support."

"I'm going with Alan," Arn said.

"I expected nothing less."

Carol gestured, lifting her companions into the air. Then she lowered the group a thousand feet, setting them on the ground in front of the Forsworn and Varjupaik soldiers waiting in the offshoot of the main canyon.

Arn saw the time-mists flow outward from Galad, swirling toward the invaders' left flank. Alan stepped into the mists two steps ahead of Arn. Kat, Quincy, Bill, and Tudor led the rest of the Forsworn in behind them.

They didn't break into a run. There was no need when the rychly mists would speed their travel, allowing them to save their energy for the battle to come.

Only Galad possessed the ability to sense what lay beyond his mists, and he brought the group out of the fog twenty paces to the rear of the Rukkumine lines. Neither Alan nor his followers uttered a yell to call attention to themselves. Alan's first stroke dropped three men before they could turn to meet the charge.

Then Arn gave himself to his heady visions of death. He saw himself die time and again, then picked a different fate, seeing a new set of futures unfold as he disemboweled his current opponent. And as he fought, a strange sense of satisfaction filled him.

The assassin whom people had named Blade was back.

—⧖—

Kim moved among the Forsworn, at the tip of the spear of the counterattack. She wielded her talent with abandon. When any of her allies suffered a wound, she funneled it through herself and into an enemy.

This use of her necrotic talent was far faster and more efficient than trying to use the life of plants to heal. But the bittersweet combination of agony and bliss enthralled her with each casting. Her longing for more grew stronger with each use of the wielding. She hated the feeling, but not nearly as much as she savored the simultaneous experience of death and rebirth. She knew that her mother would be disgusted if she could see the rapture in Kim's face as she summoned the magic, but Alan needed her skill, and she wouldn't fail him.

To her left a sword pierced Katrin's stomach just before she cut the man's throat. Kim felt the terrible tearing of stomach and intestines as she shifted the wound from Kat to the enemy soldier closing in on her.

The quick glance that Kat gave her carried the first warmth Kim had ever experienced from the woman. She didn't take the time to savor the affection.

—◊—

Commander Vrah looked about in dismay. The army of Rukkumine was in disarray. Just as his attack into the narrow pass up ahead had stalled, his enemies had launched a variety of violent hit-and-run counterattacks into his flanks. The harried reports he had received carried word of fearsome warriors with shaved heads led by a bear of a man whose great ax swept those who opposed him into the realm of the dead.

And whenever commanders believed they had these warriors trapped, odd mists would form to carry these strange soldiers to attack Rukkumine units on another part of the battlefield. Vrah knew this was false. His soldiers had allowed these foreigners to panic them into odd imaginings.

But his biggest frustration came from the witch whom his dozens of magic-wielding priests had failed to dislodge from the pinnacle on the west side of this canyon. He had gotten a good view of her through his far-glass. Dressed in an outfit that shifted colors to match the sky behind her, she was beautiful of face and body, with loose brown hair that draped the black cat on her left shoulder. But the sight of her milky-white eyes had sent a shudder through his body.

He had endured enough.

Vrah turned to his runners.

"Notify all my forward commanders that they will break through into the pass to the higher mountains or I will have their heads on pikes by nightfall. I don't care how many men they lose doing it."

—⁂—

As they traversed another of Galad's mists to get behind the Rukkumine army, Arn suffered a brief but brilliant vision of an enemy suicide assault breaking through Vahltehr's defenses, slaughtering the clansmen en masse.

He stepped up to Alan.

"We need to turn around."

"Why?"

"Vahltehr is going to be overrun."

Alan raised his left fist in the signal that brought his Forsworn to a halt, adopting a defensive posture while they waited for their Chosen to issue a new command. Arn saw Galad stride through the Forsworn toward the spot where he and Alan had halted.

"Why have we stopped?" Galad asked.

"The Rukkumine army will break through the clan defenses unless we can get there first," Arn said. "We need you to funnel your rychly fog around our enemy's western flank."

Galad said nothing, but the mists changed, a new tendril billowing out to the northwest. To anyone outside this miasma, it would look like an arm of fog racing along the side of the valley at tremendous speed. Arn hoped the sight would add to the confusion within the Rukkumine ranks. Alan led the way into this corridor, Arn and the others following him along the new path.

The valley narrowed as they neared the mouth of the canyon where Vahltehr would make his stand, leaving only one way forward, directly through the enemy troops bunched up before the entrance to the gorge. Galad's mist swept through the Rukkumine soldiers from behind, loosing Alan and his Forsworn on their startled foes.

Arn stepped into his visions of the immediate futures spinning out before him, sampling from hundreds of outcomes to guide his attacks.

He spun among three opponents, killing two, only to have a sword spill his entrails on the ground. Time and again he watched himself die as he strode through this dreamscape in thrall to his time-sight. But among the many paths to defeat, he discovered others that carried him to victory. Arn found himself growing more comfortable navigating the hallucinatory worlds unfolding around him as he fought his way through the enemy throng. The correct choices began to stand out from the others, and Arn realized that he wasn't tiring as quickly as before.

In the real world, he moved through the battle chaos with an easy grace, using subtle shifts of his body to allow weapons to glide past him while each of his counterstrokes delivered a killing blow.

—◊◊—

Vahltehr took the cut high up on his chest, then caved in the invader's head with his hammer. He was familiar with being out of the potions that made him and his men beyond superb. Now they would fall back on merely being fearless and unrelenting. They would win here today or they would die. Honor demanded nothing less.

The added pressure of knowing that their wives and children would be slaughtered by this scum if he failed did not make him fight better or worse. Uteseny, the mother of his children, would be proud. He and his clansmen were already giving their best.

His thoughts turned to his eldest son. Tudor should be here fighting alongside his father, who had already seen his other two sons fall in combat on this day. Vahltehr would grieve later. Tudor had abandoned his people to join the outsiders who pledged their oaths to the man they dubbed the Chosen. Vahltehr had allowed it. His son was a grown man, entitled to choose his path.

A yell pulled Vahltehr's eyes to his left. The Rukkumine soldiers were swarming over the bodies of their dead to gain the ledge upon which the battle hinged. Another swing of his hammer added to the stinking pile. He looked at the masses stacked up behind the wave of attackers and knew that this would be the day he died. And when he fell to these swine, so would everything he had ever loved.

Something new drew his attention. A fog like that through which he and his clansmen had traveled to reach the canyon formed and just as suddenly dissipated. And from those mists a few dozen warriors hurled themselves into the fray.

Vahltehr's heart sank. Not enough to make any difference in the outcome.

He swatted another foe from the ledge, surprised to feel the press of enemy soldiers shift as they turned to meet these newcomers to this fight. Suddenly the clan chief heard a low moan rise above the sounds of combat. Then he spotted the cause. The Chosen was carving a path through all who stood in his way with such violence that he left a wake of severed torsos.

And with him came his Forsworn, dealing death in almost the same abundance as their blood-drenched Chosen. Vahltehr recognized another of the bald warriors. Tudor. His son's face was a mask of fury, his spiked battle hammer raining destruction.

The moment the attack on this ledge faltered, Vahltehr boomed his battle cry, which launched his hundreds of surviving fighters into the enemy.

"For Rodina!"

Then he leapt from the ledge into the crimson fray.

—⁂—

Fire and ice rained from the sky onto the ledge atop which Carol stood. The elementals under her control deflected the assaults into the midst of the Rukkumine army spread out below her. One by one she ensnared the ethereal beings that her opponents used to attack her, ripped each from its former master's control, and followed the mental link back to the enemy wielder. When her mind pierced that of her opponent, she burrowed inside, taking control of the other and forcing them to rain death on their own soldiers.

Carol ignored their mental screams of agony and frustration and ended the battle of wills by destroying minds, letting dead bodies crumple in place. Then she turned her attention to a group of wielders who formed a tight circle around a lone individual.

The priests abandoned their attempts to attack her and concentrated their talents on erecting a multilayered mystic shield. Over what? The better question was: Over whom? The answer formed in her thoughts. These wielders protected the Rukkumine army's commander.

Carol raised her arms to the sky, summoning Lwellen to send dark clouds boiling into the heavens. Chain lightning crawled through the clouds, building in blue-white intensity until Leles's hair stood on end. Unable to contain the mighty charge, the clouds sent lightning downward into the Rukkumine masses. The thunder that followed shook the canyon.

Below her the army of Rukkumine roiled in panicked confusion. All it needed was one more push.

Carol summoned Ohk to lift her high in the air as she illuminated herself with a brilliant glow. With one final gesture she lensed the atmosphere, magnifying herself until she seemed to tower over all those gathered in the valley below. She spread her arms wide above her head, lightning arcing between her palms to form a dazzling orb of energy. Carol flung the bolt, energy quickly striking the shielding summoned by the priest-circle. The balled lightning exploded, sending bolts of electricity crawling through the nearby mass of soldiers, turning some to ash and others into shrieking human torches.

The army of Rukkumine broke and ran, many dropping weapons in their quest to escape the blind witch. The priests and the man they sheltered fled along with the rest.

Although she knew Arn wouldn't approve, Carol let them go.

Alan knelt beside Bill's corpse, wiping away the wetness that ran down his own cheeks with his filthy right hand. The first of his Forsworn. The young ranger had been at Alan's side in every battle since the protectors had thrown their tens of thousands against Areana's Vale. Bill had helped Alan and the women of Val'Dep hold the wall against thousands of vorgs. And he had been Alan's dearest friend.

He took a deep breath, stood up, and stepped aside to allow Quincy and Kat to pay their own respects. They and four others were all that remained of his Forsworn company.

Vahltehr walked among his wounded as the woman from Endar healed them one by one, sucking the life energy from the surrounding trees and plants, leaving only desiccated husks in her wake. The chief shoved aside his revulsion at this abhorrent use of life magic. The Endarian princess had saved many of his warriors' lives on this day. Who was he to question her methods? His own injuries would wait until after she treated every one of his warriors.

He noted that the Chosen did the same.

The clan chief now understood why Tudor believed in the legend. Vahltehr counted himself fortunate to have been here on this day to watch the greatest combatant he had ever witnessed. The faces of the Rukkumine soldiers who faced the Chosen would remain painted in his mind until the day he died. Hardened fighters had looked like frightened children as they watched the burly warrior butcher their friends before turning on them. After that they'd just looked dead.

If not for his duties to his clan, Vahltehr would have taken the Forsworn oath as well. The mountain gods knew that the Chosen needed more followers. Only six of the bald fighters had survived this day's battle. The Chosen had roamed the killing ground with them, collecting his dead and carrying them back here. When their corpses had been laid side by side, the man had knelt before each of his dead, head bowed, his scarred face etched with sorrow.

Vahltehr shook himself from his reverie and turned to his own duties. Of the thousand-plus clansmen he had led into combat, four in ten had fallen. Tonight he would allow his survivors to rest. On the morrow, with the magic of the mist-wielding Endarian speeding the journey, he would return the slain to their families. Only then would he grieve.

PART III

Though it pains me, I can allow myself no sympathies for those who will perish in order to bring to pass that which must be. Only through the crucible of conflict can the portal be opened.

—From the *Scroll of Landrel*

14

Jogi
YOR 415, First Day of Autumn

In her blue nightgown, Queen Afacere paced through her bedchamber and onto her moonlit balcony, barely aware of the chill in the early-morning air. Yesterday's news had upset her so that she found it impossible to sleep. Her city looked ghostly in the pale light. The few lamps that were lit resembled lonely glow bugs. Her eyes shifted to the southwest, as if she could discern the threat that gathered in the distant mountains that lay in that direction.

Her emissary in Rukkumine had sent word confirming the worst of the rumors that preceded his message. Kalnai clansmen, allied with the ravager they called the Chosen, had defeated that city's army. Once again Kragan had proved himself prophetic. The Chosen and his blind witch would come for Jogi next, seeking the sacred time stone and the artifact locked within.

After the defeat of the army that King Godus had sent to kill him, the other clans would flock to the call of the Chosen. What chance would Afacere's army have against him once he gathered thousands of mountain warriors?

The city was thick with tales that the man was a demigod, sent from the land of the dead to gather Landrel's holy artifacts and return them to the master of the deep. Nonsense, of course. Nevertheless, Afacere could not shake the feeling that a seed of truth lay buried in the rumors.

Afacere lifted her hands to her lips, interlacing her fingers to still the trembling. She could not allow her city to be overrun by barbarians. She had to heed Kragan's urging, despite the priesthood's opposition to the wielder's counsel.

Decision made, she turned her back on the cityscape and opened the door that led out into the hallway. She gestured to the rightmost of the two royal guardsmen stationed there.

"Send my handmaidens to me."

"Yes, Highness."

She stepped back, closed her door, and walked into her dressing room. Once the serving women clothed her, she would give the orders that would put her army on the march. Afacere would not wait for the Chosen to gather his horde. She would hit him before he had time to recruit the clans scattered throughout the Kalnai Mountains.

And she would act on Kragan's other words of advice. Afacere would send emissaries to her brother, King Troc, in Vurtsid. The king would join forces with her in Queen Severak's northern stronghold of Paradiis. There they would secure Landrel's holy artifacts.

Somehow the act of making these decisions calmed her. Time and again Kragan had proved his value to her. Only the priesthood, with its paranoid urgings that this small man was using mind magic to manipulate her, had deterred her from taking full advantage of Kragan's wise advice. The queen weighed her clerics' concerns and found them wanting. As of today, she would inform her court that Kragan would be elevated to queen's counselor, replacing old Otrava.

—✣—

Kragan, wearing the freshly tailored black uniform that denoted his position as queen's counselor, strode into her throne room with an air of belonging there. After all, it was not that long since he had been chief adviser and wielder to that fool King Gilbert of Tal. Now Kragan wielded an army through this young queen.

A worry crept into his mind, one that he tried and failed to suppress. Carol Rafel, terrible in her dead-eyed beauty, and the assassin who was somehow linked to Landrel's prophecy clawed their way into his dreams.

But Kragan held tightly to the visions that Landrel's Scroll delivered to him. The buzzing of these gnats was nothing to him. Carol Rafel and Blade would fall in the midst of the destruction that he would unleash upon this world. As for this supposed Chosen, he was merely a pawn for the master of the game to manipulate.

Kragan visualized this mighty warrior leading tens of thousands into battle against Queen Afacere's army. Yes. This would happen as Landrel intended. Odd that Kragan's purposes and those of Landrel seemed to have aligned. Was this merely coincidence? He could not bring himself to believe that. Thousands of years ago, he had killed the ancient wielder. Thinking back on his greatest accomplishment, Kragan recalled the look of surprise on Landrel's face as he died.

Odd.

Was it really astonishment he had seen in the Endarian's eyes? Or was it anticipation?

Kragan stroked his chin, pondering as he approached the queen.

"Ah, Kragan," Queen Afacere said, her worry lines relaxing at his presence. "I was about to summon you."

"Majesty."

Kragan climbed the step stool and took the seat that she'd ordered set at her right hand, beside the throne. When he proposed this arrangement, she'd welcomed the idea. But her decision had sent the rest of her court into a furious frenzy that Kragan enjoyed.

With him at her side, Afacere snapped her fingers, and the captain of her guard ushered in Otrava and General Prikazca. The white-haired adviser and the statuesque military woman both knelt before her.

"Rise," Afacere said. "What business brings you before me, General? I expected you to be readying the army for the march."

"I requested that she accompany me to this audience," Otrava said.

"You assume too much."

"My queen, it was not that long ago that you sought out my counsel. I merely seek to let you weigh guidance that differs from the diminutive one's recommendations."

"You question my decisions?"

"No. I question your adviser's undue influence. He wields subtle magic to tip the scales."

"Leave me, before I have you dragged from this chamber."

Kragan placed his left hand on the queen's arm. "Please. I would like to probe the arguments he and the general have come to make."

The queen's scowl did not leave her face, but she assented. "As you wish."

"General," Otrava said, "please express the concerns you raised with me."

The woman's stern mask had remained firmly in place since she entered the chamber. It did not break now. Kragan could well understand how she had risen to her position of authority.

"It is madness to strip this city of defenders with all the turmoil that this so-called Chosen has unleashed on Rukkumine. This may be what he seeks to accomplish."

"Have you spoken to our emissary from that city?" Kragan asked.

"I have."

"And did he not tell you that the clansmen that defeated Rukkumine's army numbered fewer than two thousand?"

"He did."

"And many of those clansmen died in combat."

"Yes."

"Yet you somehow believe that such a small force can rapidly gather the support of the various clans dispersed throughout the Kalnai Mountains to threaten this city."

"We need to plan for that possibility."

"What do you propose that Queen Afacere do?"

"Send a fresh ten thousand to finish what Rukkumine started while keeping the bulk of our forces here to defend this city."

"You would send the same number of troops into those mountains that the Chosen just defeated with the help of only one clan?"

"I've never believed that King Godus instilled the proper fighting spirit in his troops."

Kragan laughed. "Fighting spirit? That is the secret ingredient that will carry your ten thousand to victory?"

"You mock me?"

"My dear general, I do not mock your caution. But restraint will not carry the day against the Chosen. It will only demonstrate to the clans that we fear to fully engage him. That feeble act will unite them as he alone may fail to accomplish."

"I have heard enough," Afacere said. "General Prikazca, return to your command and get them ready to march."

The general bowed, then turned and walked out of the throne room. Otrava stood rooted in place. The queen turned her glare on him. Kragan recognized the moment.

"This one spreads dissension in your court," he said, "as surely as he has in your army."

"My queen, I—"

"Quiet," she said. "I will deal with you in my own time."

Once again she snapped her fingers.

"Captain, take this man from my sight and put him in a cell to await my judgment."

"As you command."

Kragan watched the guards drag the old man from the chamber, a warmth spreading through the wielder's chest. The old fool had sabotaged himself. His punishment would send a message throughout Jogi.

Everyone would know who tugged the true strings of power.

15

Rodina, Southern Kalnai Mountains
YOR 415, Early Autumn

As dusk fell, Carol watched as the last of the four chiefs, with his druid high priestess and his guards, arrived in Rodina. Unfortunately, only half of the clan chiefs had agreed to come to this meeting. It had taken weeks for Vahltehr to arrange this gathering and several more days for all four leaders to arrive from their dispersed strongholds.

Galad had proposed using his time-mists to gather the group much more quickly, but Vahltehr vetoed the idea. There was already too much suspicion between some of the clans to think their chiefs would willingly put themselves at risk with such unknown sorcery.

Carol spent much of the intervening time helping Arn practice his time magic, working on his ability to use the skill in combat. The near futures he saw were bright and sharp, and his actions had an immediate impact on how they played out. She rehearsed alongside him, linking their minds so she could test how her actions could alter what was about to be.

Hearing footsteps, Carol turned to see Kim approach, a frown on her face.

"What's wrong?" Carol asked.

"Those deep-spawned druids."

"I thought you weren't going to let them bother you."

"Yes. But they do."

"What have they done now?"

"As the newcomers arrive, Saman huddles with her counterparts from the other clans."

"Ah. Spreading word of the wielder of forbidden death magic and her sister, the blind witch."

"They call me upir."

"Vahltehr will see that the other clan chiefs learn differently."

"The way those women watch me . . . I want to rip their eyes out."

"Arn is aware. If they try to hurt either of us, he will know and stop them before anything bad happens."

"You're sure?"

Carol reached up to stroke Leles on her shoulder.

"I am."

But as she said those words, she saw Saman standing with three of her druids within a shadowed copse. The crone and her devoted followers stared at Carol, their eyes seeming to bore into her. The old woman's grin turned her face into a death mask. Carol didn't need to touch Saman's mind to know that the druids wanted to murder her and her sister.

As Carol turned and led Kim away from the watchers, her lips formed a silent response.

"Good luck with that."

—⚇—

Vahltehr walked into the meeting hall where the other four clan chiefs waited. He walked the line to clasp hands with each in turn. Horsky wore a warm smile that seemed to fit the robust body that his liking for stout ale had given him. Revat was the opposite. A slender man with a brown beard and eyes that matched, he never smiled in Vahltehr's presence. Like Vahltehr's, Vojak's weathered face showed years of exposure to the sun and chill mountain winds.

The last chief, his mane of flaming hair draping his shoulders, wrapped his thick arms around Vahltehr in a hug that strained his ribs. Vahltehr slapped Vesely on the back, motioning everyone to take a seat in the circle of chairs.

"I hear that your high priestess is at odds with you," Revat said.

"Saman is displeased with my recent actions and disagrees with what I am about to propose," Vahltehr said.

"A fact that our priestesses have already made clear to us," Vojak said. "Why have you allied yourself with outsiders and users of unnatural magics?"

"I judge people by their actions," Vahltehr said. "These outsiders have proven themselves true to me and mine in combat. They helped us drive ten thousand Rukkumine invaders from our lands."

"What of this man who calls himself the Chosen?" Vojak asked.

"Those who have sworn fealty to him have bestowed that name," Vahltehr said.

"And you deem him worthy of it?"

"I have never seen his like in battle. He strikes terror in the hearts of all who stand against him."

"If you have already defeated Rukkumine's army, why have you summoned us to a war council?" Vesely asked.

"Our scouts in the north have reported the army of Jogi is on the march. They are skirting the east side of the Kalnai Mountains."

"We know that," Horsky said. "So long as they stay out of our lands, we don't care."

"Normally I would agree. But we have reason to believe the Jogi troops have been sent to destroy the Chosen and all who stand with him."

"Fine," Revat said. "Expel this Chosen and his ilk from your lands."

"I owe him a blood debt."

"But we do not," Revat said.

"I am asking you to fight alongside me, not him."

"Why should we do that?"

"What do you think this new army will do if it conquers my lands? Just go home? No. They will have a foothold in clan lands. Do you think they will stop there?"

"I, for one, do not," Vesely said. "They will roll us up one at a time."

"Together we defeat them before they gain purchase in our mountains, or clan by clan we die."

Vahltehr looked from one to the other of the four chiefs, meeting each pair of eyes.

Revat stood up.

"I will not risk my clan in a fight aimed at this Chosen. You have wasted my time."

He stalked from the longhouse, slamming the door behind him.

"I will fight at your side," Vesely said.

"As will I," Horsky said.

"And you, Vojak?" Vahltehr asked.

"Before I make my choice, I would like to meet this man you call the Chosen."

Vahltehr stood.

"Fine. Follow me and I will introduce each of you to the man to whom a quarter of my clansmen have sworn a death oath."

—⁊⁊—

Alan watched as his followers sparred throughout the training ground in near darkness. After the battle with Rukkumine's army, more than two hundred of the clan warriors had joined the Forsworn. All these hardy and experienced mountain warriors had shaved their heads after swearing their oaths to him, these promises given with Vahltehr's blessing.

Vahltehr approached across the moonlit field, accompanied by three of the clan chiefs. Alan turned to meet them.

"Chosen," Vahltehr said, "I want you to meet my fellow clan chiefs: Vesely, Vojak, and Horsky."

Alan clasped wrists with all three as they studied him with a combination of interest and skepticism.

"Why do the druids despise you?" Vojak asked.

Alan had expected the challenge.

"They don't like the magic my wielders employ."

"I hear it's unnatural magic like that used by the priesthoods of the sea goddess, and other magics even more foul," Vojak said.

"Whether magic is good or evil depends upon the purposes to which its wielders put it," Alan said. "My sisters and Prince Galad used their talents to help us rout the Rukkumine army that invaded clan lands."

"Not according to our priestesses," Vojak said.

"Your priestesses fear losing their exalted status. They see my wielders as a threat. Thus, so am I."

"Are they right?" Vojak asked.

Alan stepped closer to the man who reminded him of Vahltehr.

"I threaten my enemies. I hope to have you as a friend."

For several moments no one spoke.

"Well said," Vojak responded.

A laugh from the redheaded clan chief, Vesely, preceded a hearty slap on Alan's back.

"Vahltehr. I judge this young cave bear worthy. He speaks truth few would dare say to us."

Alan turned to Horsky, watching as the rotund man studied him. "And what say you, Clan Chief?"

"I shall not embrace you until my eyes have beheld you in combat," Horsky said.

"Then you intend to fight alongside Vahltehr against this new horde that marches south?" Alan asked.

"Should the Jogi army enter the Kalnai, yes."

—⁓—

Arn strode beside Landrel through the knee-high grass of the vast North Endarian Plains, the stiff breeze in their faces. Behind them Landrel's cottage dwindled in the distance.

"I have done it," Arn said. "Slaken has released its contents."

"Yet you fear to touch that which I have sent you."

"I have touched the finger once. It almost destroyed me and the one I love."

"You will soon have need of the shard."

"My skill is not yet sufficient to control the thing."

"You will never acquire proficiency if you continue to refuse the artifact's call."

"My intuition will guide me."

"Be certain that your instincts drive your decisions rather than your trepidation."

Arn stopped, and the taller man turned to face him, his ebony eyes shining with challenge and expectation.

"Kragan has recovered one of the shards of your trident," Arn said.

"More than one."

"Why have you arranged this?"

"Even I cannot dictate each of time's twists and turns. Your presence smudges the canvas upon which I painted these futures."

"But your far-sight penetrates that shroud."

"Time will tell."

Landrel and the surrounding countryside began to fade despite Arn's desire to maintain his connection to the master wielder. The Endarian's final words followed Arn from dream into wakefulness.

"Do not let fear keep you from what you must do."

—⁓—

Arn opened his eyes to the predawn light filtering through the doorway of a cottage. As he prepared to climb from his blankets, his eyes came to rest on Carol's cat, Leles. The sleek black body lay in the narrow opening. Arn's gut clenched as a fresh vision formed in his mind of a robed woman's gnarled hands setting a pan of warm milk just outside that door. Then she stood and carefully opened the portal a handbreadth, the silence so deep that only magic could create it.

Without realizing he moved from his bed, Arn found himself kneeling at that opening, the lifeless form resting in his hands. Sick with fury at the one who did this to hurt his wife, Arn carried Leles back to where Carol slept, carefully laying the animal on his blanket. Dreading to do so, he leaned down and gently kissed his wife's cheek, waking her.

Though her eyes opened, he knew she didn't see him. Her brow furrowed.

"Where's Leles? I don't feel him."

Then, as he took her hand, Arn felt her touch his mind.

"Oh no."

He handed her the cat and Carol hugged it to her neck, kissing the animal's head and stroking its soft fur as sobs escaped her lips. With their minds so joined, Arn experienced her grief even as she sensed his fury.

For several minutes Arn sat beside her, letting her cry herself out. When at last she sat up, her eyes locked with his with such intensity that the sudden change startled him. But the thought she transmitted made her intent clear.

"Blade, I need you."

—⚒—

Saman returned to her cottage, careful to activate her previously prepared defensive measures. The outermost layer consisted of a series of trip wires that would trigger bells to alert her of anyone who approached within a dozen paces of the isolated house. Anyone foolish enough to come closer without announcing themselves and gaining the druid's permission would deserve the suffering her mystic tinctures would inflict.

She arranged the snares at odd intervals between trees or thick bushes that channeled visitors to pass between them. When triggered, branches would spring forward to impale the thighs of the interlopers with barbs she had coated with a knockout toxin. Lastly, Saman trapped the front door and window with bulbs of acid that would rain down upon anyone who dared open these portals.

Saman did not worry about a clansman or druid making such a foolish approach. Over the decades of mastering her craft, she had established a history of violent responses to anyone who dared violate her privacy. The outsiders were a different matter. Although she had left the poisoned milk for the blind witch's cat, the act could have been done by any of the druids whom the woman's use of foul magic had offended. Nothing about that bowl or its contents could prove Saman's involvement. Besides, it was only a cat.

But that did not guarantee that one of the witch's companions might not try to take matters into his own hands.

Saman lay down upon her bed, savoring the warm sense of personal satisfaction that embraced her. The dead cat would send a message that the blind witch would not soon forget.

Her thoughts shifted to the Endarian woman who embraced another of the dark arts. On the morrow Saman intended to arrange a reckoning with that loathsome wielder of necrotic magic as well. With that pleasant thought in mind, Saman finally allowed sleep to take her.

—⚮—

Arn stepped into the night and opened his mind to the maelstrom of futures that swirled around him. Shoving aside all but the dreamscapes that might occur in the next few moments, he focused his time-sight on the clansmen who roamed Rodina's streets between the buildings and through the woods beyond. He strode a path that avoided anyone else, his silent footsteps carrying him along a meandering route and into the forest, where a lone cabin awaited.

As he neared the cottage, Arn increased his concentration. He watched himself trip an alarm bell, then stepped over the thin vine that would have triggered it. Dozens of Arns moved through the darkness, many of his doppelgängers slumping to the ground as poisoned spikes impaled their thighs. Arn avoided the traps with a trained assassin's care.

He paused five steps from the front door, new visions flooding his mind's eye. He watched himself open the portal, saw the small clay pot fall to shatter on his head. The stringent acid within blistered his face and ruined his eyes in a moment. Arn tried the window with an equally disturbing outcome. Still, one mental picture guided him forward.

Arn moved to the door and ran the fingers of his left hand across the hole where the latch pull should have been. The moonlight that sifted through the trees confirmed what his most recent vision had revealed. The druid high priestess, Saman, had removed the cord that allowed the door to be opened from outside.

Bending down, Arn withdrew a thin-bladed throwing dagger from his right boot. Ever so quietly he worked the blade between the door and the log wall. He lifted the wooden latch and did not let it fall as he slowly inched the door inward. Arn could just make out the curved edge of the palm-size clay pot that would fall with the door's next movement.

Another set of dreams blurred before him, and again he made his choice. Arn gave the door a gentle shove, stepped to his right, and delicately caught the fragile container with his left hand. Setting the pot on the ground, Arn returned the dagger to his boot, withdrew a damp cloth from his pocket, and slipped silently into the cabin.

—◊—

Saman awoke to the hands that stuffed a wet rag in her mouth and held it there. The man rolled her facedown and pinned her in place, her struggles barely audible to her own ears.

The rag tasted of milk and heavy cream. It carried a faint but familiar odor. Her fright transformed into terror. Tincture of umrtie, the same poison she'd drizzled into the milk she left for the blind witch's cat. Now her mouth was full of it. And when the man pinched her nose shut, the sense of suffocation filled her with such terror that she could not stop herself from swallowing.

What began as a burning sensation in her throat spread rapidly through her stomach and into her chest. The extract from the roots of the umrtie plant attacked the nerves, stopping the heart within moments, leaving no signs of an unnatural cause of death. Over the preceding decades, several of Saman's rivals had succumbed to her special brew.

Violent convulsions shook her body but failed to dislodge the man who held her down. Saman felt her attacker's lips brush her left ear. His words followed her into the dark tunnel that devoured her.

"The blind witch sends her regards."

—⁓—

Blade rolled Saman onto her back. He closed the druid's eyes and pulled the rag from her mouth. He lifted the pitcher from the table beside her bed, refilled the metal mug, and rinsed out the dead woman's mouth. Then he arranged her beneath her covers, letting the remainder of the mug's contents spill out onto her neck and blankets, as if she'd spit up as her heart failed her. He lay the mug as if it had fallen from her lifeless fingers.

Then he slipped through the puddle of light that the waning crescent moon spilled through Saman's window and into the night, one shadow among the many.

16

General Prikazca watched from atop a barren hillock as the thirty thousand soldiers of the army of Jogi turned west, streaming through the foothills toward the southern Kalnai Mountains. The fact that none of the scouts she'd sent up into the clan lands had reported back bothered her. The twoscore priests who accompanied her army had failed in their attempts to see deeply into the highlands.

That lack left her feeling exposed in a way she didn't like. Perhaps it was time to send forth a probing attack to discover the layout of enemy forces. As much as she hated to sacrifice a thousand troops in the effort, remaining blind to the enemy was not a valid option.

Turning to her flag bearers, she gave the order that they relayed to others who echoed the command throughout the column. As the bulk of her troops moved into defensive positions along the north-south ridgeline, her advance guard continued their march toward the mountains in the west. Commander Scuka had earned her position at the head of the elite unit, and Prikazca couldn't think of a better leader for the mission.

Now Prikazca and her soldiers just needed to settle in and wait for the advance guard to make contact. Once that happened Scuka would send a detailed report of clan defensive positions. Then the general would finalize her plan of attack.

For the next week, she waited. But when no word from her advance guard arrived by the morning of day ten, Prikazca could tarry no longer. How had none of her thousand best soldiers managed to return? As hard as it was for her to accept, her fear that every member of her advance guard had been killed or captured transformed from inconceivable to factual.

With the weather turning colder, the time for her forces to launch a full-scale attack on the Chosen had arrived. General Prikazca gave the command that put the army of Jogi on the march, aware of the aura of dread that infected her troops. Not knowing the status of her best combat unit felt worse than having seen them slaughtered.

The distant mountain pass toward which they marched drew Prikazca's gaze. Somehow the Chosen had managed to crush her soldiers' morale from afar. And no fiery speeches before her soldiers could restore it.

Though she kept all emotions from her face, she could not shake the feeling that she would never see home again.

—◊◊◊—

The enemy fought bravely, never asking for quarter and never getting it. Alan's warriors traversed Galad's time-mists to chase down the dozens of messengers who tried to return to the main body of Jogi's army with word of the Chosen's tactics. Alan lost 120 of his Forsworn in the battle against this Jogi regiment. But for each of his warriors who fell, he gained two more recruits from the clans, bringing the number of his Forsworn to almost four hundred.

While Alan and his faithful awaited the inevitable arrival of Jogi's army, he and Galad drilled them on the tactics of fighting within the time-haze. And with the help of those who were now veterans of the Forsworn, the newly pledged members quickly became proficient at the hit-and-run techniques designed to throw confusion and fear into a much larger force. Their mission was to set the enemy up for the counterattack by the four thousand clansmen led by Vahltehr and his three clan chief allies.

But tonight Alan's warriors rested. As Alan himself considered catching a few hours of sleep, Galad stepped from a moonlit tendril of mist and approached him.

"Our enemies are on the march."

"How much time do we have?"

"A day, maybe two depending on the weather," Galad said. He gestured toward the sleepers. "Do you want to wake them up?"

"No. They need the rest."

"I'll let Carol, Vahltehr, and the other clan chiefs know."

Alan watched the Endarian walk away, feeling Ty's ax on his back. The thing seemed to become more a part of him with every killing.

A motion at the corner of his eye caused him to turn his head.

"Kat."

"Why have you not made it to our bedding? The night grows chill without you."

"War approaches on the morrow."

"All the more reason to revel in this night. Take my hand. Let me show you."

"Revel?"

"Relish. Carouse. Make love. I can be more explicit."

"Yes, you can."

Alan reached out and let her fingers intertwine with his. When she led him into the copse where they spread their twin bedrolls on the thick pine needles, he shed his armor, clothing, and underthings, noting that she was quicker.

Then, as he pulled her supple body atop him, all thought of warfare faded away.

—⟋⟍—

From behind a tree, ten paces away, Kim watched and listened as the couple's low moans increased in pace and intensity. When Kat finally collapsed atop Alan, Kim slipped away with the chill night breeze.

—⟋⟍—

Carol awoke to find Arn sitting beside her, holding her hand, gently massaging the back of it with his thumb. She linked with his mind, seeing herself through his eyes. He would stay with her, letting her see the shifting tides of combat and how each of her actions would change the outcomes.

"Thank you," Carol said.

"For what?" asked Arn, genuine curiosity in his eyes.

"I have no right to expect you to be my eyes. I never thought that Leles's death would hit me this hard, but it feels like I just lost another member of my family."

Arn took both her hands in his.

"I was so focused on preventing an attack on you that I never considered that anyone would target your pet. I should have foreseen it."

"I know I need to cast off this sadness. I'm just grateful to have you beside me so that I can touch your mind."

"Vahltehr has offered you a dog to take Leles's place."

"It's too soon."

Carol took a deep breath, releasing it with a shudder. She let go of Arn's hand and sat up to pull on her boots. When the blankets fell away, the morning chill made its presence clear. Her breath puffed out in little clouds in the predawn light.

"Are you ready for today?" Arn asked.

"I will be. Any update on how long we have?"

"Galad says that the enemy's lead elements will reach this valley by midafternoon. He thinks that after sunrise you should kill any hawks or vultures we see."

"Any that I'm not using."

"The Jogi priests will be doing the same."

"Or trying to."

Arn rose to his feet, as did she. Gazing into her own white orbs, she experienced her husband's concern.

"I think you should accept Vahltehr's dog."

"No."

"I can't protect you like this."

"I do not need your protection."

"I can't be your pet."

"You're not my pet."

"Then what have I become?"

She resisted the urge to slap him, and Arn shared her emotion, his hurt every bit as vivid as if she had.

"Can you do this for me one more time?" she asked. "Just for today."

Arn paused longer than she liked. What would she do if he refused her request? His answer allowed her to take a breath.

"For today."

—⁓—

General Prikazca, surrounded by two dozen of the hundred priests that Queen Afacere had sent with her army, gave the order to advance into the first of the high passes that formed the gateways into the southern

Kalnai Mountains. Never in her long career had she felt this unsure of what awaited on the other side of those obstacles.

The narrow opening would funnel her army to the point that her front lines would emerge only a few hundred soldiers abreast. But they would be supported by the scores of priests scattered throughout the horde. Her lead elements would bear the brunt of the losses their enemies would inflict, but Prikazca intended to use the tremendous mass of her army to bore her way through the Chosen's defenses.

She welcomed a battle of attrition. In such combat the side with far greater numbers always won. The army would return to Afacere wounded but victorious. And Prikazca would personally drop the heads of the Chosen and his blind witch at her queen's feet.

—⚉—

Unlike in previous battles, Alan and his four hundred Forsworn charged into the teeth of the hundreds that poured into the pass, swathed in Galad's mists. He was fully aware that Carol's magic couldn't penetrate the mists, but then neither could that of any priests who hadn't yet entered the fog that swaddled the Forsworn.

Alan knew that the enemy saw a dark fog race into them. The first ranks would feel as if they crawled from the muck into a place where the mists around them cleared, revealing the rush of bald warriors who crashed into them with a violence that shocked the Jogi soldiers.

Not all Alan's followers were clansmen, and those few who weren't didn't partake of the druidic potions with which the clan warriors enhanced themselves. Kat and Quincy fought to either side of Alan, allowing space for his whirling ax to rend and shred the bodies of his opponents. He hammered into the mass of those who stood before him, the tip of the spear that his Forsworn drove into the chest of this invading army.

As the clash of steel on steel and the howl of screams became a cacophony of death, Alan gave himself over to the moment.

—ᨆ—

Sergeant Lovec watched as the unnatural wall of mist raced into the chasm through which he and the other soldiers that formed the Jogi front line marched. He expected to die as the foul magic engulfed him and his fellows.

The wall of fog passed, revealing hundreds of charging clansmen led by a bald hulk whose ax felled three soldiers in a single stroke. Lovec knew that he beheld the one these people called the Chosen. A bald woman ducked under Lovec's sword to strike at him with a long knife, its blade glancing off his shield and missing his throat by a fingerbreadth.

Lovec stumbled over a stone that twisted his left ankle, his fall saving him from her follow-on attack. A booted foot caught him in the ribs, sending him rolling. His head struck another rock, narrowing his vision to a pinpoint. But if he lost consciousness, he might never regain it. The sergeant blinked and realized that his eyes must have been closed for some time. He shoved aside the pain that blossomed in his skull, sucked in a shuddering breath, and slowly extracted himself from the bodies that lay piled atop him.

His vision cleared to reveal a scene that shocked him to his core. The mists were gone, and he was alone. Thunder rumbled through the gorge as lightning crawled from the dark clouds overhead. The bodies of the dead were strewn all about, the corpses piled several deep across the hundred paces that separated the cliff walls. He turned to see that the carnage extended around the bend from which he and his fellows had come.

By the sea goddess, the impossible had happened. The Chosen and his clan supporters had driven the army of Jogi back out of the narrow pass.

Despite the throbbing in his head, Lovec's thoughts began to clear. The rumble in the canyon was not solely that of thunder. Sounds of combat echoed from the distant bend beyond which the rest of Jogi's army yet battled.

Lovec surveyed the battleground. Something was wrong with what he was seeing. He didn't know how long he'd lain here among the dead, but where were the rest of the clansmen? This pass should be filled with many hundreds of clan warriors who would have followed the Chosen through the pass. It made no sense.

And then it did.

He turned his gaze toward the bend in the gorge beyond which the sounds of combat echoed. A dread whisper escaped the sergeant's lips.

"Oh no."

—⚏—

Carol stood beside Arn atop an invisible platform she'd created. Through her husband's eyes she watched the battle play out in the forests and glens below the pass from which Alan and his Forsworn pushed the forward lines of Jogi soldiers.

More importantly, she observed the ghostly futures that Arn's time-sight revealed, casting spells in the now to alter impending outcomes. The Jogi priesthood had sent many magic wielders with this horde, and without Arn's foresight they might overwhelm her.

Alan's plan was a bold one, fraught with such risk that the clan chiefs had almost rejected it. But Arn's support convinced Vahltehr, and he'd persuaded the other three to agree.

The entire tactic hinged on the violence with which the Chosen and his Forsworn would hammer the Jogi front lines. The bulk of the clansmen lay hidden inside a magically concealed canyon on the Jogi army's southern flank. Taking advantage of the confusion created when

Alan pushed the Jogi forces out of the high pass, Carol rained destruction on the central mass of their enemies.

The chiefs led four thousand potion-maddened clansmen charging into the southern flank of the Jogi army.

Despite her best efforts to protect her allies, the forces became so intermingled in roiling conflict that she couldn't separate friend from foe. So she focused her attacks on enemy troops not yet engaged.

More of the priests now centered their attacks on Carol, forcing her to channel most of her elemental magic into protecting the ledge where she and Arn held sway. With a shift in her meditative state, she dimmed her sense of the visions that flooded through her link to her husband. She stood in a vast emptiness, across which bright points of magic rippled outward like hundreds of pebbles tossed into a still pond.

Most of the disturbances in the blackness were widely distributed. But a cluster drew Carol's attention to a distant point around which they bunched. Of all the enemy wielders, these gave off the most intense vibrations.

Carol let the meditation fade as she directed Arn's gaze to search out Alan. He wasn't hard to find. Despite the relatively small numbers of the Forsworn, the battlefield swirled around them like a whirlpool. And at that maelstrom's center, a combination of white pomaly and dark rychly mists surged and eddied. She tried to reach Alan's thoughts within the fogs but then remembered that no type of mind magic, be it elemental or psychic, could penetrate a time-mist barrier.

Frustrated with her inability to pass information about the location of a key target to her brother, she considered another alternative, a perilous one. For it to work she needed to replace her mental connection to Arn with a link to something that would let her see the battlefield.

Through Arn's eyes she searched her surroundings, now and in a host of immediate futures. Suddenly she spotted the squirrel in a knothole, high up on a nearby pine. She established a gentle link to the creature, feeling its terror as it huddled inside its hiding place.

"Arn."

"Yes?"

"I need you to take a message to Alan. I've found a replacement for you here."

She felt the eagerness that her message spawned within him.

"What is it?"

Carol placed the image in Arn's mind of the elite group of priests clustered on a wooded knoll northeast of Alan's position.

"The priests are protecting someone important there. I can think of only one person who would require so much arcane protection that I can't penetrate it."

"The army commander?"

"Yes."

"I will deliver your message."

"I can't protect you within those masses."

"Then I guess we get to find out how well I can wield my time-sight in combat."

"Be careful, my love."

"Careful won't get it done."

As much as she didn't want to admit it, Carol knew that he was right. She switched the full power of her mind link from Arn to the squirrel. The animal's little heart was beating fast, and Carol soothed the beast's mind, then forced it to emerge from its hole and climb to one of the highest branches.

She surveyed the killing field, this new perspective improving her ability to shield her position and target those who attacked her. If only one of the clustered priests would try to kill her, she could establish a link to that person and force him to attack the others. But there appeared to be no such fools in the tight group. For now, Carol would have to content herself with fighting the rest of the priesthood present within the valley.

—⁂—

With Slaken in his right hand and a dagger in his left, Arn slipped through the forest, feeling free for the first time all day. Hearing the clash of weapons accompanied by the grunts and cries of desperate combat, he narrowed the focus of his time-sight until it merely augmented the intuition he'd relied upon his entire life.

He wondered if he could increase that ability by taking the mummified finger from the pouch at his waist, then rejected the idea. No good could come of losing himself in the madness the thing generated within him.

Arn shook his head to clear it. He needed to maintain his goal of finding Alan but stay in the moment, examining the nearest futures to find a path that would take him a few steps closer to his objective.

Two men crashed into Arn. Slaken took the throat of the rightmost, but his impact caused Arn's dagger thrust to miss the man on his left. The sword removed Arn's left arm at the shoulder, unleashing a river of pain that dulled his sight.

Arn rejected that path in favor of another where he sidestepped the combatants, thrusting Slaken into the back of the first man's neck before jabbing his dagger into the eye of the second. He dragged the latter into a dense thicket, taking several cuts from thorns in the process.

He needed only moments to strip the man of his Jogi uniform and chain mail. Arn pulled the clothing on over his, topping it with the dead man's bloody chain shirt and helmet. Then he made his way out of the dense brush and onto the battlefield, moving away from where the thousands of clan warriors fought, burrowing his way into the disarray that consumed the ranks of the Jogi army.

Everywhere he looked, he saw confusion and dismay on the faces of soldiers who saw their army assaulted from two directions. A thick fog flowed down from the ridge he'd just descended to engulf Arn and everything around him, reducing visibility to three paces. This held no trace of the time-mists that Galad wielded. Arn mentally saluted his wife.

He felt the need to get to Alan tug him forward, allowing the dreamscapes he sampled to guide him along the path of least resistance. And where he met opposition, he killed and killed again.

—ᴍ—

General Prikazca watched the shimmering haze of priestly defensive shields across which the blind witch's lightning skittered and clawed. The way some of the senior priests and priestesses groaned under the arcane assaults concerned her. How could one being bring all this power to bear while defending herself from the scores of other wielders scattered throughout the valley?

A greater worry was the state of disorganization that cascaded through her forces like a virulent infection. First came the shock of having her lead elements enter the chasm that provided passage into the lands of the Kalnai clans, only to have them driven back by the warriors who fought within an otherworldly mist.

The clans followed this lightning blitz, launching thousands of warriors into her army's southern flank. Masked by magic, they charged into Prikazca's soldiers from the rear. These offset attacks almost split her army in half. If she could regain control of her forces, she would crush the clansmen within a mighty vise. But the competing cyclones of magic that roiled the sky and bounded across the killing ground made such control impossible.

Her flagmen did their best to forward her orders to her subordinate commanders, to no avail. Either their compatriots didn't forward her communications, or her regimental leaders were incapable of complying with her instructions.

So Prikazca did the only thing she could do in such circumstances. She sent runners to pull her two thousand elite guards in around her, packed in shoulder-to-shoulder ranks that would protect her and the priests who formed her magical bulwark.

How could so few do this to so many? It was almost as if the sheer size of her army worked against her. The thought pulled forth her childhood memory of a hawk sitting on a treetop. A much smaller bird flitted around it, screeching, diving, and pecking until the larger bird could no longer take the harassment. She watched in amazement as the larger bird fled the zone of engagement.

That option was not available to Prikazca, even if she could justify a retreat for the purpose of reorganization for a new attack. Word of her failure would make its way back to Queen Afacere. Only the headsman would eagerly welcome Prikazca's return after such a humiliation to the city-state and its beautiful young queen. Worst of all would be for Prikazca to face the imp who had become her queen's chief adviser.

That Kragan could work his way into her thoughts at a moment like this disturbed her. She had the strangest feeling that he was aware of what was happening, that he was thrilled by this turn of events.

Paranoid thoughts.

Nevertheless, Prikazca owned them.

—❦—

Alan saw the mist engulf the next grouping of enemy soldiers, transporting them from their world into his. His eyes were drawn to the priestess who began casting the spell that might end him. Unfortunately, none of his warriors was within spear or arrow range of the woman. But as she raised her arms, the smile that split her victorious face was matched by the slit that suddenly opened in her throat.

The Jogi soldier who'd slashed her neck tossed the wielder aside and yanked off his helmet.

Arn!

Before Alan could yell the order to stop, Quincy closed with the assassin, his longsword streaking toward Alan's brother-in-law's head. It didn't seem that Arn moved quickly. He merely shifted his weight, letting the weapon pass close enough to ruffle his hair. Then Arn stepped in close, clapping both hands to the sides of Quincy's face, the tips of the blades he palmed pointing straight up. A grin spread across Arn's blood-smeared face as recognition dawned in Quincy's.

Alan blocked an enemy blow with his shield, then stepped forward, his ax shrieking through the air with the howl of a soul stealer. As welcome as he found Arn's arrival, the business at hand took precedence.

He took another cut, this one deep into his left thigh. He struck out, the crescent blade shearing the shield and the arm that held it on its arc into the soldier's torso. As Alan began his next stroke, he saw an injury like his own form on his opponent, even as the wound in his leg healed. Kim stood close enough behind him that he heard her gasp of pain.

Thank the gods for the Endarian princess who accompanied his Forsworn. Despite the enmity between the two women he found himself attracted to, Alan watched Kim heal Kat just as faithfully as she did the wounds of other warriors.

Arn moved beside him, avoiding enemy blows with such grace that it seemed to Alan he knew exactly what his opponents would do before they did. Alan battered his way forward with brute force. But Blade was a surgeon, killing with a precision and ease that left Alan almost envious.

Then again, there was no greater satisfaction in battle than having your opponent accept your blow on his shield only to have that defense obliterated. The blow drove the shield into its bearer with such force that the arm that held it shattered.

"This way," Arn said, turning the fight to the southeast.

Because he trusted the killer who was his adopted older brother, Alan followed. And those who remained of his Forsworn came with him.

—⁂—

Carol watched as Galad's time-mists changed direction, the fog turning southeast as he left a wall of white haze in his wake. Since she could do nothing to directly aid Alan or Arn through the obscuration, she turned her attention toward the killing ground upon which the clans fought.

Through the eyes of the squirrel, she magnified the scene. The Jogi priests and priestesses mixed in with the army were now indiscriminately raining fireballs and lightning down on their own forces in hopes of killing the clansmen intermingled with their troops, as sure a sign of desperation as the disorderly manner in which the Jogi army churned.

Carol began deflecting the enemy spells into the ranks of their own soldiers behind the front lines. If she couldn't penetrate the mystic defenses of the tight group of priests who surrounded this army's commander, then she would extract a price in blood from the rest of the priests.

As she'd hoped, a few of the wielders turned their spells on Carol. But the minds of the priests couldn't encompass the mystic power that she brandished. One by one she wrested control of the elementals from the priests, following the link back to the mind of an enemy. Rather than grant them the peace that came with death, she severed the priests' connections to their own bodies. And as she shifted from one caster to the next, they crumpled to the ground amidst their fellows, living but worse than dead.

She took no pleasure in the act, which produced the intended effect on the soldiers near each fallen priest. They rushed in to help their holy ones. Finding the clerics alive but unresponsive, troops carted them away from the fighting, further disrupting the military cohesion of their units.

And as their frontline priests collapsed, so did the enemy's morale. Sensing the change in momentum, the potion-crazed clansmen redoubled their efforts, turning the battle into a slaughter-fest.

Fleeing Jogi soldiers turned their weapons on any of their countrymen who tried to inhibit their retreat.

—⟋⟍—

General Prikazca stared out over the war zone, dismay filling her heart. Her army seethed, stirred by twin prongs penetrating its heart from opposite directions. The Chosen's blind witch eviscerated the priests that Prikazca had sprinkled throughout her army to support her troops with magic. The results were now obvious for all to see. Military discipline and order dissolved, and unless Prikazca did something extraordinary right now, the battle was lost.

She inhaled and issued her order in a voice loud enough for the group of elite priests and priestesses who surrounded her to hear.

"Drop your shielding. Strike the witch with every sliver of ability you possess. Hold nothing back. Kill her now or we all perish."

—⁂—

Carol felt the disturbance in the ethereal planes as the group of priests defending the Jogi general shifted from defense into a coordinated attack focused solely upon her. Without Arn here to warn her of this assault, the magical battering ram severed her link to the tiny squirrel, incinerating the animal in an instant.

Blind and unable to generate a counterstrike, Carol put all her will into strengthening the bubble that shielded her. But the damage was done. Thunder shook the ground beneath the ethereal platform upon which she stood, even as a collection of earth elementals tried to liquefy the stone upon which Alan and his Forsworn fought. She shifted her focus, simultaneously linking her mind to five of the beings that tried to undermine her footing. With an effort that exceeded any she had thus far expended, Carol took control of the elementals, forcing them to defend the spot where she stood. The effort siphoned away her reserves and left her shaking.

Carol whispered the request that she knew Arn couldn't hear.

"By all the gods, I pray you have foreseen this."

—⁂—

Blade fought his way through the elite soldiers who guarded the enemy general, dodging killing blows he saw coming seconds in advance. He threw daggers, one after another, at soldiers who tried to hurl spears at Alan, then plucked his weapons from their throats or eye sockets.

The Forsworn were so close to reaching the circle of priests who were about to launch a synchronized assault on Carol that Arn could no longer constrain himself to remain near Alan. The Chosen drew so much enemy attention fighting within the time-mists that his advance wouldn't reach the priests in time to save Arn's wife.

So he ducked away, emerging from the leading edge of the rychly mists to rush forward, his visions solely directed at bypassing the general's guards, not bothering to kill those who struck out at him. Swords, maces, and spears missed him by a hairbreadth. Blade accepted minor wounds to speed his assault.

He slew the first of the priests as he sensed Carol's defenses failing. The robed men and women were so tightly bunched that each of his movements killed another. Several attempted to shift their magical attacks to target him, only to find that he shielded himself behind their fellows or was no longer in their line of fire.

The disruption he delivered allowed Carol to seize the mind of one of her attackers and use him to attack the other frantic priests. In doing so she freed Arn to target the slender female commander of Jogi's army. The general drew her saber as Blade closed the distance that separated him from her. She was quick. Blade was quicker. He shifted his weight, feeling the breath of air her stroke generated on his cheek. Then he buried Slaken deep in her stomach, the strength of his thrust driving its tip into her heart.

Behind Blade, Alan led his Forsworn out of the mists, his great ax singing on the wind. The immediate futures Blade watched suddenly coalesced into a brilliant vision. As Arn hurled the general's dead body down from the promontory from which she observed the combat, Carol bathed the scene in brilliant light.

When the general's limp body shattered on the boulders below, Jogi's army broke and ran.

17

Jogi
YOR 415, Late Autumn

When the first courier arrived with the news of the Chosen's devastating defeat of Jogi's army, Kragan stoically allowed Afacere to vent her rage on him in her private chambers. When her fury gave way to depression, he spoke his first words.

"My queen, as foul as this news seems, it may contain a greater boon."

"A boon? My top general and half my army lie dead while the survivors limp toward home."

"The Chosen savaged a force of ten times his number. But he did so at great cost. He stands diminished."

"True, but my spies report that the remaining clans are now flocking to join him."

"Imagine if you had not attacked him. He would have had time to recruit those clans and would even now be marching toward Jogi. And with those added numbers, he would crush your army, destroy your city, and massacre your people."

"Now he will have an easier time of that."

"Not if we aren't here."

"What?"

"He seeks the time stones containing the three shards of Landrel's shattered trident. But you can still flee north to the fortress of Paradiis, taking the artifact, the remainder of your army, your people, your high priestess, and all the priests in the university with you."

"When I agreed to that plan, I did not anticipate that my army would have already suffered such a defeat."

"What if I can show you how to defeat the Chosen and his blind witch?"

Afacere's eyes widened in disbelief.

"How can running away lead to victory?"

"Because you won't be fleeing. You will be leading the Chosen and his followers into the jaws of a trap. And when it springs closed, the Chosen will be crushed between the combined might of Paradiis, Jogi, and Vurtsid."

"What of the other holy time stones?"

"All three will be brought together, secured within the unassailable fortress of Paradiis."

The queen walked over to her window to stare out across her beloved Jogi.

"Will the Chosen burn my city?"

"I do not know."

Kragan stepped to the window and looked up at the queen's distraught face.

"But I promise to bring you the heads of the Chosen and his witch after this is over."

She looked down at him.

"You swear it?"

"On my dead mother's corpse."

Afacere returned her gaze to the city, the muscles in her jaws tightening.

"I will send word of my plan to my brother, King Troc of Vurtsid, and give the order to my people to make ready to evacuate the city and board our merchant fleet for Paradiis."

"What of the approaching remnants of your army?"

"I will leave ships to transport them. Now leave me. I wish to be alone."

Without a word Kragan turned and walked out the door.

He did not let a grin make its way onto his face. Events were progressing precisely as he and Landrel intended.

18

Troc sat atop his cushioned ivory throne, rubbing his bearded chin in deep contemplation. When he raised his eyes to meet those of Modrost, the gray-haired woman who was his chief adviser, trepidation filled him.

"You have confirmed my sister's entreaty?" Troc asked.

"Yes, Highness. Our spies in Jogi confirm the defeat of Queen Afacere's army and the subsequent evacuation of Jogi."

"I wouldn't have thought it possible for the Kalnai mountain clans to unite under one leader, much less an outlander."

"By all accounts, this bald man they call the Chosen is a warrior such as those whom old men tell of around campfires. He has amassed an army of almost twenty thousand clansmen, hundreds of whom have shorn their heads and pledged their lives to his service."

"What of the Landrel artifacts?"

The woman scowled. "We have received confirmation that the sacred time stones have been stolen from Rukkumine and Varjupaik. I can only conclude that the Chosen has taken them."

"For what purpose?" asked Troc.

"I believe that he's turned them over to the sightless witch who accompanies his army."

"Why do you think that?"

"The survivors of Jogi's routed army report that she overcame more than a hundred of Queen Afacere's priests. She left dozens helpless cripples, despite their bodies bearing no discernable wounds, almost as if she broke their minds."

"But the shards from Landrel's Trident cannot be used. They are encased in time stones."

"The witch appears to have found a way to release them."

"Impossible."

"Our sources in Varjupaik report that the Chosen and his marauders claimed to have sailed from Endar."

"No one can sail through the time-mists that surround that continent."

"A prince and princess of Endar accompanied the Chosen."

"Endarians?"

"Yes. And if the witch was able to dissipate those mystic fogs, she may be able to dispel the time stones."

"Then it's no wonder the Chosen defeated the armies of Rukkumine and Jogi."

"It's what I fear, Highness."

"What think you of my sister's plan?"

"We cannot face the army of the Chosen alone. He must not take one more of the precious time stones."

Troc nodded in understanding. "The bastion of Paradiis."

"It offers us our best chance of safeguarding the final three of the sacred relics. And your army will stand shoulder-to-shoulder with the remnants of Queen Afacere's forces as well as the army of Paradiis."

"And," Troc said, "we can gather the combined magic of the priesthoods of Paradiis, Vurtsid, and Jogi."

"Hundreds of Dieve's disciples, including our most powerful high priests and priestesses."

King Troc leaned back on his throne.

"I am decided. The bulk of my army will make ready to sail. I shall take our holy relic to Paradiis. There we will join forces with Queens Afacere and Severak. Together we shall grind this Chosen, his witch, and the mountain clans beneath our boots."

"You will leave this city undefended?"

"Not entirely. I believe the Chosen and his army will continue their northward path toward Paradiis. My city and its people will be safe."

Modrost bowed ever so slightly, then turned and exited the throne room. Troc's eyes followed her until the two guards outside closed the doors behind her, leaving him alone. Then he took a deep breath and slowly shook his head.

A new thought kindled a slow-burning fire in Troc's gut. What foul twist of fate had delivered these pillagers to Sadamad? Why did the sea goddess permit it?

He arose, straightened his thin frame, and shoved his worries aside. When the Chosen reached Paradiis, Troc would settle the score.

19

Northeastern Kalnai Mountains
YOR 415, Late Autumn

Kim stood alone on the hillside overlooking the line of encampments that stretched for more than a league along the river that wound its way north through this wide valley. On this moonless evening, she didn't need her inherited Endarian ability to see in almost total darkness to observe what lay below her. Fires lit the campsites of the seven clans who had allied themselves with the Chosen. Only one clan had failed to heed his call to war.

Alan had lost almost all his Forsworn during the charge that killed the leader of the Jogi army. But once again new recruits had flocked to the Chosen, pledging their lives to this warrior living legend. The Forsworn once again doubled in size, now numbering more than two thousand.

Figures moved in and out of the light of the half dozen fires that lit the nearest camp. As always her eyes were drawn to Alan, sitting in close conversation with Quincy and Tudor. Kat hovered over her lover, alert for any potential threat, well aware that Kim was the most present danger.

Each time Kim traded her health for Alan's wounds, the bonds that chained Kim to her half brother tightened. The longing grew so intense that yesterday she'd failed to conceal it from him. Now that it had happened, Kim was happy Alan knew of her desire.

And during their brief moments of private contact, she saw the want in his eyes as well. Only Kat stood in her way. During the Jogi battle, Kim had struggled with the temptation not to heal Kat of a possibly fatal wound. It would have been easy to target her life magic on saving another of the Forsworn.

For several weeks Kim had avoided establishing the mental link she and Carol could share. But she thought her sister knew her innermost feelings. Alan wasn't the reason Kim avoided their psychic connection. Kim could sense the seed of darkness that grew within her with each use of necrotic life magic. She could remember hating the idea of killing another sentient being. Now she found herself enjoying the expunging of one life to save another. Her mother had warned her, and Kim dreaded the thought that Carol would discover her secret.

Unwilling to watch Kat any longer, Kim turned away from the scene and slipped deeper into the night.

—⁓—

Carol felt the big dog's wet nose press against her naked back, awakening her from her late-afternoon nap. She ignored the gentle prods from the animal that had become her beloved pet. More than that, Zaislus was her friend. Carol had slept the night away with her head resting on Arn's left shoulder. Not wanting to wake him, she merely reveled in the opportunity to enjoy her husband's peaceful slumber.

The changes these last few weeks had wrought in him thrilled her. The supremely confident and dangerous man she had fallen in love with had returned in full force. Day by day, Arn's use of his time-sight during sparring sessions improved.

With her mind linked to Arn's, she stayed in the background as a silent observer, careful to avoid distracting her husband as he practiced his magical talent. This evening he had Tudor as his sparring partner. Instead of their using sticks against each other, Arn wanted to test his skills in hand-to-hand combat against the larger clansman. As Arn circled he saw Tudor lunge for the takedown before it happened. Arn sidestepped the tackle and delivered a glancing blow of his fist to the side of his opponent's head. Tudor shrugged off the punch, wading through a hail of quick jabs that bloodied his nose and lip.

The vision storm within which Arn operated dizzied Carol. Although she continually pushed him to practice using the artifact from Landrel's Trident to see farther into the future, he refused, determined to master his time-sight's combat capabilities first. As she watched him scan hundreds of scenarios in a moment, Carol marveled at how far he'd progressed in such a short time.

Tudor bull-rushed Arn, who dropped to the ground, avoiding the clansman's grasp and sweeping his legs from underneath him. Tudor hit the ground chest-first, his breath leaving his lungs in an explosive gasp. Arn landed hard on the bigger man's back, driving the rest of the air from his lungs and locking his right arm around Tudor's throat. As Arn locked his choke hold into place and tightened his grip, Tudor slapped the ground twice in surrender.

Arn released his sparring partner and climbed back to his feet. Tudor rolled onto his back and lay there, struggling to recover the breath that his fall had knocked out of him. Arn smiled and extended a hand to the fallen warrior, helping him back to his feet.

"What just happened?" Tudor asked, wiping the blood from his nose and mouth.

Arn thumped him on the back and laughed.

"I got lucky."

"Since you started beating Quincy, you seem to get lucky a lot."

Carol released her mental link to Arn and reconnected to her new canine companion. Through the dog's eyes, she watched the two men grip forearms. When Tudor turned and stalked back to the Forsworn portion of the camp, she shifted her gaze back to Arn.

The decision she'd made during the Jogi battle to release Arn from her mind link had been a good one. His accusation that she had been using him as her pet was difficult to accept, but it was true. And thus she'd reversed course and accepted Vahltehr's gift of the waist-high hound she named Zaislus.

She heard the pine needles rustling in the wind and the squirrels skittering from limb to limb as if the sounds were magically amplified. Together these sensations enraptured her.

Most of all, Carol loved Zaislus's protective nature. Each morning, in stark contrast to Leles's aloofness, her dog welcomed her to wakefulness with such joyful anticipation that she couldn't help hugging him, ruffling his fur, and smiling as she had seldom done since her blinding. Zaislus liked Arn, tolerated Alan, but eyed most others with an aggressive wariness that made it clear they were on probation.

But her dog's dislike of Kim shocked Carol. Despite Carol's admonitions, Zaislus's hackles rose and his lips curled into a snarl that rumbled from low in his throat whenever Kim made an appearance. Worse, the dog's distrust of her half sister was so intense that it took considerable force of will for Carol to calm him.

Arn's voice pulled her from her musings.

"Are you hungry?"

"Starved."

"Good. I smell food cooking."

His words pulled her attention to the scent. The vivid smell of mutton roasting on a fire pulled forth a rumble from her stomach.

In the twilight she took Arn's hand and walked to the nearest of the cook fires with Zaislus at her side. Moments later, their plates filled with healthy portions of beans, she seated herself beside Arn among a group of Forsworn who encircled the dying embers.

Quincy stepped up to the fire and bent down to drop an armful of sticks atop the coals. One of the thicker limbs landed awkwardly, its tip launching a smoldering ember high into the air and down the neck of Quincy's leather jerkin.

With a yell he stumbled backward. His vigorous attempts to untuck his shirt funneled the cinder into the seat of his pants. Quincy dropped his trousers. Pants around his knees, the lanky swordsman tripped, sprawling face-first into a mud puddle. Ignoring the howls of mirth from all onlookers, Quincy rolled over and lay back, letting the cold water soothe the blisters on his backside. Having watched the antics from Zaislus's bemused viewpoint, Carol laughed until tears streamed down her cheeks to drip from her chin. Just when she got herself back under control, a chortle from Katrin brought forth a fresh round of guffaws.

When Carol was finally able to finish her dinner, she gave the scraps to Zaislus, then turned to walk with her husband back to the spot where they had made their camp. She and Arn spread their bedrolls beneath a towering pine. With her head resting on Arn's chest and Zaislus resting at her feet, she smiled and drifted into the first pleasant dream in many weeks.

The chill in the predawn air awoke her. Carol extracted herself from her husband's arm and sat up, awakening Arn in the process. With Zaislus's eyes, ears, and nose she scanned the copse that sheltered them.

"You're up early this morning," Arn said, rising on one elbow.

"You didn't dream last night."

"Maybe Landrel is tired of bothering me."

"I doubt it."

"I'll take a good night's sleep whenever I can get it."

Carol climbed from her bedroll, the chill in the morning air making her glad that she had slept fully clothed.

"How long will Alan wait for Clan Chief Revat?" she asked. "Do you think Revat will bring his clan to the war camp?"

"I don't know. When I get better at foresight, I'll try my hand at looking more than a half day ahead."

Carol dressed herself in her durable Endarian uniform. When she pulled on her boots, she found that they weren't quite frozen, just cold enough to be uncomfortable. She summoned a fire elemental to create a ball of flame that hung two feet above the ground. Whenever she summoned Jaa'dra, the detailed image branded into her shoulder throbbed, the pain a lingering aftereffect of the moment when Kragan had helped the ethereal being overcome her.

"Ah," Arn said as he finished pulling on his own boots and extended his hands to the warmth. "Occasionally I forget how handy your magic can be."

"Enjoy it while you can. I think I'll see if Alan is up. I want to ask him the same question I posed to you."

Arn pulled on his black shirt, strapped his knife and throwing daggers to his body, and turned toward the distant clearing where the Forsworn camped.

"I may not have foreseen the precise moment, but I think your brother is anxious to get his army on the move. He won't wait much longer."

As she led Arn out into the broad clearing, Carol didn't disagree with Arn's assessment. Her need to stop Kragan from gaining any more of Landrel's artifacts made her want to get the pursuit started. But right now, she wanted to hear Alan's plan firsthand.

—◊—

Alan arose so silently that he didn't awaken the woman who shared his blankets. The dull glow of predawn hadn't yet begun to light the eastern sky, but he awakened with a nervous energy that required him to start moving. After dressing, he walked out into the clearing around which a few dozen of his Forsworn pulled guard duty.

Quincy was the nearest guard, and Alan returned his hail as he walked by. He headed toward the activity around the fires being lit near the cook wagons, only to be intercepted by Arn, Carol, and her dog.

"How much longer do you plan on waiting for Revat to show up?" Carol asked.

Alan didn't miss the impatience in her voice.

"If I don't get any word from the last clan before sunrise tomorrow, I'll order the march."

"Good."

"Today I'll tell the chieftains to prepare their warriors to break camp. Tomorrow morning we will march northwest across the southern Jogi plains."

"How many do we have with us?"

"A little more than two thousand Forsworn," Alan said, "thirteen thousand clansmen, ninety-seven druids, a few dozen Varjupaik soldiers, and a couple hundred wagon masters, blacksmiths, cooks, and other tradesmen."

"Can Galad wield the mists required to speed so many?" Carol asked.

"He was able to enclose more than twenty thousand of Father's legion."

"Yes, but he overtaxed himself. That effort cost him his left hand."

"Father's legion became too geographically spread out in those rugged canyons," Alan said. "The number of soldiers wasn't the problem. The distance across which they were spread defeated Galad. This time we will tightly pack the clans to facilitate our journey through the mists."

"Channeling that much time magic worries me."

"Galad says he can handle it."

"And he can," Arn said, "but I would advise you to make frequent stops. It will allow our scouts to reconnoiter while Galad and your warriors rest."

"That will slow our progress."

"Better to be fresh than flagging when we encounter our enemies."

"Your visions have confirmed this tactic?"

"No."

Carol placed a hand on Alan's forearm.

"No one wants Kragan dead more than me, except for Arn. But we should *not* underestimate the forces he'll throw at us."

Alan weighed his sister's words, knowing that every day of delay lent the foul wielder another opportunity to gather yet another of the shards of power. However, the fact that Arn also urged caution decided him.

"I will tell Galad to advise me whenever he needs rest."

"Thank you."

Alan left the two of them, feeling the urge to find an isolated place where he could be alone and clear his mind before dawn delivered its ceaseless tasks. He climbed a thickly wooded hillock, only to bump into Kim as she rounded a tight turn in the narrow trail. She stumbled and would have fallen had he not caught her and pulled her into his arms.

She leaned into him, the act unleashing a torrent of desire that he didn't try to resist. Her arms circled his neck as her parted lips met his. With his breath coming in ragged pants, he sank onto the pine straw while her hands roamed his heated body, her Endarian clothing so silky smooth that it was as if she weren't wearing anything. Within moments, neither of them was.

The wrongness of what they were doing skittered around the edges of his mind, but somehow only enhanced their passion. Alan's yearning became an ache that yielded to ecstasy that he wanted never to end. But when it finally did, they lay together, Kim's long hair cascading down on his sweat-soaked face and neck.

When Kim lifted her head to look down at him in the first pale light of dawn, she placed her fingertip across his lips, signaling silence. His eyes devoured the curves of her form as she dressed. Then she smiled down at him and departed.

Alan finally sat up, running his hands across his smooth scalp.

"Well, Chosen," he whispered, "you have a knack for finding trouble."

20

Jogi
YOR 415, Late Autumn

Carol watched as Alan swept into the abandoned city of Jogi at the head of his two thousand Forsworn. His clan warrior allies followed them into the city. He gave strict orders that the elderly and other poor people who remained in the ghost town not be harmed. That message didn't go over well with some of the clan chiefs, but Alan remained adamant. There would be no slaughter of innocents on his watch.

The clans searched the city, making sure that no enemy troops remained hidden within. Alan and his Forsworn surrounded the huge building at the city center, intending to secure the temple that the Varjupaik commander told him he would find within.

Carol, Zaislus, and Arn walked through an arched entry into the expansive central square. A sea-green temple occupied the center of an exquisitely landscaped park that covered the area enclosed by the massive building that bounded the quadrangle.

Carol halted outside the massive doors.

"It's as beautiful as Varjupaik's temple," Arn said.

"But not a replica. Let's find the altar."

Carol felt the reluctance that crept into her voice. She expected that the Landrel artifact would be missing but dreaded the confirmation that awaited her.

When Arn pushed open one of the towering double doors, Carol was amazed at the ease with which the thing swung inward on its hinges. She stepped inside. The interior was dimly lit by sunlight filtered through the high, seascape-painted windows.

With a thought Carol lit the hundreds of candles atop the white altar at the large room's center. Somehow that light seemed more appropriate for this place than that of a glowing elemental orb. A glance confirmed her forebodings. The cornerstone was missing.

"Kragan now has another of Landrel's shards."

"Not necessarily," Arn said. "If he's further augmented his magic, I believe he would already have made another attempt on your life."

"He would have to be close enough to see me. Without his link to Charna, he would have had to face us in combat."

"Then why would Kragan convince the merchant queen to abandon her city without a fight?"

"Haven't any of your dreams or visions given you a clue?"

"Landrel showed me this moment, but nothing beyond now. I think he wants me to do something."

Arn walked to the altar and knelt, rubbing his hands around the edges of the hole the time stone once occupied, as if his touch might guide his time-sight. After several moments he slowly shook his head. Then he sat down cross-legged before the altar and untied the small pouch from his belt.

Carol stepped up behind him.

"Are you certain you want to try this?"

"We need to know what Kragan is up to."

"Shouldn't I link our minds together first?"

"I need to do this on my own."

Carol sat down beside her husband, facing his left side. Suddenly Zaislus's eyes focused on the ear that had been sliced to a point during one of Arn's battles. She reached out a hand to stroke Zaislus's head, as if the dog could soothe the worry that robbed Carol of her voice.

Arn dumped the bag's contents on the marble floor, took a deep breath, and then grabbed the mummified finger with his right hand.

—���—

The brilliance of the light that blossomed around Arn made him shield his eyes with his left hand as he clasped the fragment of Landrel's Trident in his right. His ears ached from the cacophony that bombarded him, and his skin felt as if he rolled in a bed of a thousand needles. Sweet aromas wafted through his nose, immediately replaced by smells so foul they left him nauseous, the air so thick with odors that he could taste them.

What was happening? The temptation to drop the artifact grew so strong that Arn opened his clenched fist to release it. At least he tried to open his hand. But cramps froze his muscles so tightly that his body might as well have been transformed into stone.

A familiar voice whispered in his ear. Landrel's.

"You have entered a temporal nexus, experiencing a deafening chorus of untold futures. Follow me and live, or remain here and die."

Through bleary eyes Arn saw the slender Endarian's ghostly figure emerge from the dazzling background. Landrel moved past him without pausing and began to disappear back into the haze from which he'd appeared.

With an effort unlike any he'd ever sustained, Arn forced his tortured body to rise. He stumbled after the ancient wielder, barely managing to keep him in sight. And as he moved forward, bit by bit the sensation storm subsided to a dizzying blur. Landrel's image clarified, and Arn's muscles loosened. Soon he found himself striding alongside the taller man as the world changed around them.

They stepped out onto a battlefield strewn with the bodies of clansmen and olive-skinned soldiers, some of whom wore Jogi army uniforms. But most of the dead were unfamiliar. In the distance smoke rose above a walled city as tongues of flame licked the evening sky. The visions of near futures that Arn had begun to master churned before them. Landrel chose one and Arn followed him into it.

Their ethereal forms stood inside a large vault between rows of piled treasure. On the far side of the room, Kragan stood beside a white pedestal from which a pale mist flowed. When that transient fog dissipated, the wielder reached for the three objects that the dissipating haze revealed.

"No," Arn yelled.

He drew Slaken and rushed the man he had spent his life hunting. His blade plunged into the back of the wielder's neck. Kragan did not hear him, did not feel the ghostly thrust.

Kragan's right hand closed on the three skeletal fingers atop the pedestal, while his left clutched the three fingers that dangled from his necklace. When Kragan thrust his fist skyward, tendrils of shadowed magic curled around it.

Landrel gestured, freezing the scene that had just played out before them.

Arn turned on the Endarian, frustration clenching his fist.

"This will happen?"

"Yes," Landrel said.

"Can I change it?"

"My time-sight grows hazy where you are concerned."

Arn gestured toward the frozen Kragan, the thrill of victory etched into the evil wielder's face.

"Then why is this so real?"

"You see it in detail?" Landrel asked.

"Perfectly."

Furrows wormed their way across Landrel's forehead. As Arn opened his mouth to speak the question that leapt to his tongue, his vision dissolved into mist, taking the long-dead master of the nine magics with it.

—◊—

Carol saw Arn drop the shard from Landrel's Trident and open his eyes. The scowl on his face told her that something hadn't gone well. She placed a hand on his arm.

"What is it?"

"I lost myself again. Landrel found me."

"And?"

"He led me to Kragan."

"Where?"

"Inside a vault. I don't know where."

"What disturbed you?"

Arn met her gaze.

"From atop a table, Kragan grabbed three of the fingers from Landrel's Trident. He wore another three on a necklace."

Carol's chest constricted. The number filled her with dread.

"We have only one of the mystic shards. If Kragan comes to possess six of the nine, we're all doomed."

"I think that's why Landrel wanted me to experience this waking dream. Just before my vision ended, he looked worried."

"And I'm right there with him."

PART IV

Dark or light, each by itself is nothing. But when one such as I masters both aspects, the fates themselves can be altered. Thus shall I revise my future and the destinies of all whom my weaving touches.

—From the *Scroll of Landrel*

21

East of the Sienos Range
YOR 415, Early Winter

Alan ordered the army of the Chosen to make camp just southwest of
the spot where the rugged Sienos Range pinched a narrow strip of flat-
lands against the northern tip of Jogi Bay. The map King Trgovec had
given Kim indicated that this was the primary overland access to the
plains southeast of Paradiis, the city toward which Arn's visions summoned them. Winter's arrival blocked all passes through the mountains,
so this was the sole route to their objective.

The necessity of tightly grouping his almost twenty thousand warriors so that Galad's time-mists could enclose all, along with Alan's
mandate for frequent stops, slowed their movement.

"The smell of a fight is in the air," Quincy said.

"A big one is waiting for us beyond that passage," Alan said.

"Then why do we wait here?" Vahltehr asked. "All this stopping
gives our enemies more time to prepare for our arrival."

"It gives our scouts a chance to reconnoiter what awaits us north
of the Sienos Range," Quincy said. "And these stops have allowed your
druids time to prepare more doses of their potions."

"I prefer violence now rather than a timid advance."

"A blind rush is useless. They know we are coming. Haste will not produce the advantage of surprise."

"They cannot see our formations through the time-mists."

"No, but they will see the dark fog racing toward them."

"What of it?"

"The remnants of Jogi's army will have shared their experience fighting within the mists with the army of Paradiis."

Vahltehr laughed.

"And," Quincy said, "they'll have scouts atop the mountains looking down on our advance. The shape and size of the time-mist will reveal how we're bunched."

As the two men whose counsel he had come to value argued for their desired strategies, Alan regarded them. The graying clan chief preached aggressive use of high-risk, high-reward tactics. The tall swordsman favored caution and planning. Despite their differences, the two were close friends. And their disagreements provided Alan with the pros and cons of each approach, aiding his decision making.

Alan raised a hand.

"Enough. I've made my decision. We'll make our final preparations for battle in this camp. Tonight, Galad will accompany a handful of our best scouts, speeding their journey into the mountains. Once they've gathered knowledge of the enemy that awaits us beyond the pass, we'll finalize our assault plans."

"And then?" Vahltehr asked.

"Galad will summon the mists within which we will wheel around the eastern tip of the Sienos to unleash a frenzy of destruction such as our enemies have never faced."

"I don't like it. I think we're becoming too predictable."

"Noted."

Vahltehr turned and walked away. Alan felt Quincy clap a hand on his shoulder.

"Don't worry. I know Vahltehr. He'll have the clansmen ready."

Then the swordsman strode down toward the site where the Forsworn were making camp. When Alan started to follow him, Kat stepped from behind a tree to confront him.

"Have you bedded the Endarian?"

Alan stopped. Kat stepped close enough to touch him.

"Have you?" she asked.

"Yes."

"You share the same father."

"It was a mistake I will not repeat."

"But you enjoyed it," Kat said.

"People enjoy many things that cause harm."

"I have chosen you. I will not share you with another, especially not your sister."

Kat whirled and disappeared into the woods. He had the feeling that his moment of weakness with Kim wasn't the only disastrous mistake he might be making.

—✲—

High Priestess Svaty stood beside Klati, the commanding general of their combined armies. Together they looked at the tens of thousands of soldiers who waited on the Paradiis Plain. They were leagues northeast of the narrow passage through which the Chosen's army would round the easternmost tip of the Sienos Range. The army of Paradiis composed the majority of the anvil against which the enemy would crash. But Queen Afacere provided another ten thousand fighters, the survivors of Jogi's ill-fated invasion of the Kalnai Mountains.

Queen Afacere's greatest contribution to the combined army was her high priestess's commitment to lead the hundreds of clergy who populated the university that Svaty headed. The queen remained behind, within the fortified walls of Paradiis, along with the wielder who had Her Majesty's ear.

Svaty extracted a fist-size crystal globe from the folds of her robe. The water-filled device that Kragan had created still amazed her. Using unknown magic, this sphere linked to its twin, which remained in the Zvejys wielder's possession. When both were uncovered, each scrying orb allowed its possessor to see and hear the surroundings of the other.

Right now the scryer showed only darkness.

"Kragan," Svaty said.

For several moments nothing happened. Then the cloth that covered Kragan's crystal lifted to reveal his face.

"Yes?" Kragan asked.

"Our scouts are flashing mirrors to signal the rapid approach of the fog that concealed the Chosen during the Kalnai battle," Svaty said.

"Has General Klati thoroughly briefed all his commanders about how the time-mists affect those who fight within them?"

"Yes, and they have spread the word to every soldier."

"What of your priests?" Kragan asked.

"All understand that no magic can penetrate a mist barrier. They will stand ready when the mists engulf them, revealing our enemies within."

"The Chosen's mist wielder may also dispel his time-mists once the front lines of the two armies become entangled," Kragan said. "Most likely, he will use a combination of these tactics to generate confusion and isolate portions of our army."

"You never told me how you came by such detailed knowledge of the Chosen and the wielders who have accompanied him from the continent of Endar," Svaty said.

"How I know this is none of your concern."

"Understanding how you attained this knowledge will help me trust your motives."

"Your queen trusts me. Take care not to anger her."

The orb went dark as Kragan replaced the covering on his. Svaty stared at the crystal for several seconds, working to restore her calm. Kragan should be out here avenging the slaughter of his fellow villagers instead of whispering in Afacere's ear, safe within the fortress of Paradiis.

A dangerous question formed in Svaty's mind: What game was the Zvejys wielder really playing?

—⚬—

Kim moved through the time-mists alongside the Forsworn with the grace that only an Endarian could command. She knew that of all the battles in her life, the biggest was on her doorstep. She hungered for it. To taste death and life simultaneously filled her with such an intoxicating mixture of pain and pleasure that her desire for more immersion couldn't be denied.

Her eyes found Alan, and once again she felt his hands on her body as she moved atop him. Though he didn't yet know it, he was her Chosen. Kim would push Kat aside. The woman was a favored member of Alan's Forsworn, but she wasn't the crucial piece of the Chosen's destiny. Only one who could wield magic such as Kim's would fill that role.

Galad's yell brought her back to the present.

"Attack!"

A dozen paces ahead, armored soldiers bearing unfamiliar crests struggled from a zone where time passed more slowly. Alan and his Forsworn hurled themselves into the fray, misting the air red. Quincy took an arrow in his stomach, and Kim absorbed the worst of the wound, transferring it to the archer as she rushed to the fallen swordsman's side. She placed her right boot on the man's chest and pulled the arrow free, finishing her life energy transference.

Glorious. She needed this.

Alan was a god of death, cloaked in the blood and gore that his ax sprayed into the sky. And every injury he suffered Kim shared, strengthening her bond with her lover. In an ecstasy surpassing all but what she'd experienced in Alan's arms, Kim funneled the injuries of dozens through her body and into her enemies. She died and lived a hundred times, a thousand.

A heavyset female soldier struck at Kim, opening a wound from left shoulder to elbow. Kim smiled and exchanged the wound with her attacker. Tudor took a possibly fatal blow to his head and Kim transferred the injury to the woman who'd cut her arm, relishing the taste of that soldier's life as the woman passed from this world into the next.

A vivid memory of the young girl she had been when she first used this forbidden ability wormed its way into her mind.

—⁂—

A movement in the bushes brought Kimber's head around. She whistled and was rewarded by a happy yelp as a large golden-haired beast bounded from the nearby thicket. Kimber knelt to wrap her arms around the dog, laughing as its long tongue licked her face.

"Leala," she said, "I've missed you too. Show me those pups of yours."

But as she rose to follow the dog back into the thicket, a familiar voice brought her to a stop. "Hello, Kimber."

She spun to see Erelis, an older Endarian boy who had asked the queen for permission to court her. Despite Kimber's objections, Elan had given Erelis her permission. Kimber knew why. Erelis was the scholar that Elan wished her son, Galad, was, and the queen was thus blind to the suitor's shortcomings. Despite his handsome face, something about Erelis greatly repelled Kimber, and yesterday she'd made that fact plain to him.

"You followed me!" she said, letting her fury fill her voice.

Erelis stepped forward, surprising her when he grabbed her hand and pulled her into an embrace. She tried to pull away, but he was stronger; his breath came in ragged pants. He tripped her and fell to the ground atop her body, pinning Kimber. She tried to strike out at him but could not free a hand to do so. His face lowered toward hers, and she turned her head away. It didn't matter. She felt his hot breath and lips on her throat and screamed, her mind reeling with disbelief that this was happening. But this far into the woods, there was no one to hear her cries.

But then Leala was on Erelis, snarling as she grabbed his leg and pulled. With a curse, Erelis released Kimber and kicked at the dog. When Leala did not let go, Erelis grabbed a thick stick and struck the dog in the face, sending her tumbling away. His face contorted in fury, and he rose to his feet, putting all his strength into a blow that put out an eye and dropped Leala to the ground, bleeding from the mouth.

"No!" Kimber screamed as Erelis raised the stick to deliver another blow.

Fury misted Kimber's eyesight as she called upon her life-shifting talent, knowing that what she was about to do was forbidden. Forming the channel, she funneled her own health into the dog, accepting Leala's agony as terrible wounds formed on Kimber's body. Her consciousness tried to fade, but she would not allow that to happen. Instead Kimber completed the channel, extracting the life essence that she required from Erelis.

She ignored his screams. His actions had revealed the ugliness that rotted his soul. The shifting cycle continued until both she and Leala were made whole once again.

Erelis collapsed to the ground, his hands clutching at his crushed eye. His shattered jaw tried to form words but merely managed a mewling sound. For several moments Kimber stared down at what she had done. Then she turned her back on the grisly sight and ran.

—ᴍ—

Kim forced her way back into the chaotic world of battle. She spotted Galad attacking an enemy with his sword even as he wielded the time-mists around them. Whereas moments before she had been able to see the vast expanse of Alan's army, only the few thousand Forsworn now occupied this stretch of condensed time.

Just as in the last battle, Galad had released Carol and the clansmen into the realm where time passed normally so that they could engage the bulk of the enemy army, enabling Carol to wield her magic in all its vast power. The gambit also allowed Galad to enhance the speed with which the Chosen and his Forsworn could move, much like a cavalry unit, thrusting at their opponents at places of Alan's choosing.

But there was a change that surprised Kim. Arn wasn't with the Forsworn. That could mean only one thing. His time-sight perceived a danger to Carol that forced Blade to remain at her side instead of using his ability to guide Alan's thrusts.

To Kim's left front, Kat gutted a man, but suffered a puncture that severed her heel tendon and dropped Alan's lover to her knees. Kim embraced the wound, opening a necrotic channel into the spearman who'd hurt Kat. When he stumbled forward, Kat cut his throat and resumed her place at Alan's left flank.

Kat gave no thankful nod. Amid all the death and destruction, there would be no time for such a nicety. Still, the omission irked Kim. She stored the kernel in a distant corner of her mind and continued performing the magic she had been born to wield.

—ww—

Carol was surprised when Arn chose to remain at her side as the time-mists dissolved around them and tens of thousands of clan warriors. The clansmen, high on druidic potions, hurled themselves into lines of enemy archers and pikemen, quickly becoming so intermingled that the battlefield roiled in chaos.

Seeing through Zaislus's eyes from his precarious perch atop the gnarled trunk of a fallen oak, she scanned the field of battle as thunderheads boiled into the sky above.

Carol cleared her mind, entering the meditative state in which she could see the elementals that others summoned to the killing field like burning brands in a dark cavern. So many flames came to life that it reminded Carol of the candles atop the altar she had seen in Dieve's temple inside Varjupaik. And from those hundreds of sparks, magic arced toward the clansmen, uncaring that they were intermixed with the armies of Jogi and Paradiis.

Carol's mind snapped outward, calling forth her own army of elementals to counter the attacks, creating a bubble across which lightning and fireballs skittered. And where the earth elementals tried to liquefy the stone and soil beneath the feet of the clan warriors, she transformed the topsoil into diamond-hard crystal.

Vahltehr formed a ring of several hundred of his elite guard to protect Carol. Blade prowled among them, her lion, guided by his visions of the future, preventing any puncturing of that barrier. Already he was drenched in blood.

Carol studied the way the Jogian and Paradiisian priests probed her defenses. Hundreds of the wielders sent the elementals they controlled skittering across the shielding that she'd erected. Carol found their efforts wanting . . . and that caused her some concern.

King Trgovec of Varjupaik had told Kim of Jogi's university. All five of Sadamad's city-states sent their acolytes there to be trained in the magics. When deemed ready, they returned to their home temples to use their talents to serve the sea-goddess, Dieve. And Kim had passed along that knowledge to her sister.

Those who sent forth these feeble attacks were acolytes. Her question was: Why? Where were the high priestesses, the priests, and their seasoned brethren in this fight? If they were thinking to have their trainees tire Carol, they were misinformed.

As she puzzled on this, a bigger question loomed over her. Where was Kragan?

—⁓—

The wielder roamed the streets of Paradiis, carefully noting the location of all its defenders. More important, Kragan wanted to understand the presence of the priests who remained within the fortress-city. Queen Afacere had told him the history of Paradiis, the paranoia of its progression of inbred merchant queens having led to the construction of high walls and fortifications.

Unlike any other of the five city-states on Sadamad, a king never ruled Paradiis. These people considered it sacrilege against the goddess Dieve to allow a man to rule. While Queen Severak tolerated Kings Troc, Godus, and Trgovec, Queen Afacere was the favorite of her counterparts.

Kragan had always wondered why the master of the nine magics had allowed Kragan to kill him. Landrel welcomed that death, had placed his right hand on Kragan's forehead as he died. Kragan would never forget the far-off look in the Endarian wielder's eyes, nor the hint of a smile on his lips as he crossed into the land of the dead.

But it was Landrel's final eight words that had haunted Kragan through all the centuries.

You still have a role in my destiny.

Kragan had not understood the statement, but now he stood on the verge of such knowledge.

When he reached the Paradiisian Temple of Dieve, Kragan walked up the thirteen steps that led to the turquoise-inlaid double doors. Those doors now stood closed. Kragan turned his back to them and looked out over the expanse of the central square.

It was one of the most beautiful sights he had ever seen. Flower gardens wove intricate patterns through the lush grass of this park.

Blue-green paver-stone walkways wound through the expanse that surrounded the temple, connecting scores of ornate fountains. Above all the natural beauty, storm clouds spun an arcane web of lightning. Thunder rattled the doors.

Well beyond this city's outer wall, the Chosen and his army were driving the combined armies of Paradiis and Jogi back toward this stronghold.

Kragan turned, opened the rightmost door, and stepped into the chamber that housed Paradiis's Altar of Dieve. He shut the door behind him. Whereas the other temples that Kragan had visited were festooned with paintings of the goddess and the sea, this one was monochromatic, the walls, ceiling, and floor covered in turquoise tile, producing the illusion that you were swimming beneath a calm, sunlit sea.

The color scheme also served to direct worshippers' attention toward the white altar illuminated by hundreds of dancing candle flames.

Three cerulean-robed priestesses formed a triangle around the sacred shrine. Two stood behind the altar and one stood centered at its front. All three faced the door, their arms crossed, hands hidden within their sleeves. The colors of their vestments blended so well with the rest of the room that their faces seemed to float in the air.

The closest of the priestesses spoke in a tone so low that it was almost lost in the rumble of the distant thunder.

"What purpose brings Queen Afacere's adviser here?"

"I merely wish to kneel before Dieve's altar in supplication."

"What boon do you seek from our goddess?"

Kragan spread his arms.

"Nothing that we do not all desire. Victory over the pillager who calls himself the Chosen."

"Then you may depart by way of the door through which you entered. We have already communicated that prayer."

"Surely all are welcome to pay homage here."

"Normally. But in times of great crisis, only the holy triumvirate shall stand watch."

"Since I am here representing Queen Afacere, may I not kneel at the altar's base and place a hand upon it? Will you deny her that courtesy?"

The woman's sharp features appeared to harden, but she gave a single nod.

"Do not linger."

Kragan walked to the right corner of the dais and knelt, head bowed. He did not pray. His gaze took in the cornerstone, the same milky white as the other time stones that composed the altar. This didn't surprise Kragan.

The ship bearing King Troc and his sacred relic had arrived only yesterday. The relic lay secured alongside that of Queen Afacere within the royal vault. The time to reunite this cornerstone with its sisters had not yet come. Kragan reached out and placed his hand on the time stone above the one that held his attention.

He rose to his feet.

"Thank you."

Then he turned and exited the temple. Outside, the noon sky grew dark and the peal of thunder sounded closer. He took one last glance back at the temple, then turned and made his way out through the park. For now, he could afford to be patient.

22

Ledinis River Crossing, Southeast of Paradiis
YOR 415, Early Winter

Carol looked across the wide but shallow river crossing. Hundreds of bodies floated downstream, tinting the water red. Most of those corpses floated facedown, but some were merely torsos, shorn of arms, legs, and heads. The scope of her brother's success in this campaign eclipsed any the Chosen had thus far achieved.

The enemy armies had retreated through the Ledinis River at great cost. And after they made the crossing, the Forsworn and the clans had harried them with such ferocity that they gave the armies of Paradiis and Jogi no chance to stop and regroup.

But Carol had her share of worries. She'd expended more energy than she thought crushing the hundreds of acolytes and junior priestesses whom the rulers of Jogi and Paradiis threw against her. A memory blossomed in her mind.

Her father, High Lord Jared Rafel, had taken her on a hunt when she was four years old. They passed by a river beside which a half dozen deer were grazing, just as a swarm of insects descended on the animals, driving them into such a frenzy that they plunged into the rapids to escape the tiny creatures.

Carol had watched the biting flies sweep all these magnificent animals to their deaths. The sight had horrified her such that she had never forgotten it. Now she swatted the acolytes who harassed Alan, the Forsworn, and the seven clans. But she took no pleasure in the killing of novices.

Where were the more experienced magic wielders, and why were they staying out of this fight?

She lensed the air before her, pulling the distant parts of the battlefield closer as if she looked through a magnificent far-glass. The mists within which Alan and his Forsworn struck, pulled back, and struck again confused the armies they faced. Thousands of clan warriors waded into the enemy with such berserk fury that their foes fled the field.

Something was wrong here. In all the battles that Carol had been a part of, when the front lines of an enemy tried to break and run, they jammed up against their comrades who were trying to get into the fight. Here the enemy's rear ranks fell back in an orderly manner, letting the wounded and frightened pass through, as if they wanted to entice the clansmen forward.

She shifted her gaze to Arn, watching as he dodged the blows of everyone trying to get at him, cutting them down with startling efficiency. Carol established a mental link to her husband and watched his visions illustrate all possible short-term futures that could directly affect him or Carol. She spoke her thoughts into his.

"Something bad is happening."

"Where?"

"On the wider battlefield. I do not know what or why. I need you to look farther ahead."

Arn killed the soldier who sought to impale him on a short spear, then disengaged from the combat and ran to Carol's side.

"I'll try."

Arn's visions branched and extended, some blurring more than others as he examined one after another of the less immediate futures, searching for the most probable. His focus shifted to one that pulled a gasp from Carol's lips.

Tens of thousands of troops wearing unfamiliar uniforms and armor rushed from the southeast, trapping the army of the Chosen between them and the forces that Alan and the clans now battled. Carol dropped her mental link to her husband. She didn't need to see more of what was shortly going to happen.

"Can you find us a way through this?"

For several moments Arn didn't reply. When he did, his words killed all hope.

"I can't see a path that gets any of us out of this alive."

—⟁—

Surov, the commanding general of the Vurtsid army, rubbed his hands together as he studied the distant battle through his far-glass. After his army disembarked from the hundreds of ships that composed the Vurtsid fleet, he'd force-marched King Troc's army from the northern tip of Jogi Bay. His soldiers were now closing on the army of the Chosen from behind. The trap had already been sprung.

He merely needed to give the signal that would tell the armies of Jogi and Paradiis to commit to this fight all the forces they currently held in reserve. That would unleash the mightiest priests and priestesses on the continent. While it was unfortunate that thousands of allied soldiers would die along with the Chosen's horde, there was no help for that.

General Surov turned to High Priest Bhakta.

"Send the signal."

The slender old priest reached out with both hands, turning his palms up. A purple flame formed above them, then shot up into the sky. It exploded a thousand feet overhead, shooting violet streamers that arced back toward the ground in a display worthy of royalty.

Moments later an answering display erupted over the distant walled city, this one blossoming brilliant red.

The Vurtsid war chant began within Surov's elite guards and quickly spread throughout his army. The general could not have suppressed his smile if he'd wanted to.

—⟴—

Fighting within the time-mists, Alan didn't see the fireworks that initiated this change, but he and his Forsworn felt the results. Suddenly an enemy they had forced into retreat counterattacked. It surprised the Forsworn so that, for a handful of moments, their lines faltered. Alan hurled himself into this breach, his howl of fury accompanied by the clamor of his ax. He yelled at Galad.

"Dispel the mists. Let the rest of our enemies see me and my Forsworn."

With a gesture Galad complied. The mists dispersed on the wind, revealing the extent of their plight at a glance. An unknown army charged into the rear ranks of the clansmen, cutting off any chance of retreat. The curse escaped Alan's lips as he looked around for new options.

"Deep-spawn."

Lightning lanced down from the black clouds to arc across the shielding that Carol erected. Alan felt the ground lurch beneath his feet, then still, as his sister stifled the elemental that tried to undermine him.

Alan spotted Carol as she, Arn, and Zaislus rose into the sky to hover over the killing ground, drawing all eyes to her. She spread her hands, summoning a pair of fireballs so bright that Alan couldn't stare directly at them. One shot toward the army that attacked from behind him. It streaked across the sky to hit a magical shield that shimmered and then shattered with a boom that dropped hundreds of soldiers to the ground.

Her second fireball launched along the same path as the first. Meeting no arcane resistance, it tumbled through the advancing formations, leaving behind a path of smoldering corpses and burning vegetation. A cascade of sorcery rained down on her. The bubble that encased her platform glowed a brilliant orange, but it didn't fail.

"Good girl. You've got their attention."

Making his decision, Alan turned, leading his Forsworn along a new path he cut through the ranks of those who blocked his way to Carol and the thousands of clan warriors who surrounded her. He saw her look toward him and knew that she understood what he intended. If they were to have any chance of victory, the Forsworn needed to reunite with the clansmen.

He charged, his bellow of rage drawing the eyes of the enemies who had not yet faced the Chosen. And as he waded across the corpses of those who fell before him, those eyes widened in shock.

—ɯ—

Kim watched Alan lead the hundreds of Forsworn who still lived into the flank of the newly arrived army that sought to block the Chosen from reuniting with the clans. He fought with a rage that his body seemed barely able to contain. Male and female soldiers alike fell to the horrifying ferocity of his blows. She saw the fear in the faces of those who would be next to fall to this bear of a man who waded through blood to get at them.

The Chosen's rage infected his Forsworn followers. Kim felt it fill her soul until she became a willing plague bearer. She wielded her necrotic magic with utter disregard for her own safety, reveling in the exchange of life and death with which she healed friends and murdered foes. A thick-bodied soldier impaled Quincy, and Kim sucked the life from him as he pulled his blade from her friend's stomach, savoring the taste the transference left on her tongue.

Her vision misted into shades of red. Healthy bodies glowed bright orange, while the wounded shifted toward the dark end of the red spectrum. She extended herself beyond any limits she'd previously experienced, healing and killing multiple targets simultaneously. But she found that she couldn't keep pace with the numbers that Alan was sending into the land of the dead. Neither could she heal as fast as needed when members of the Forsworn fell.

She began to see the transference of life energy, ghostly tendrils sprouting from her victims to funnel through her and into those she saved. Wounds crawled across her body, healing as fast as they appeared. Kim saw the looks of horror cross the faces of Forsworn who watched her and understood. She was practicing a most malevolent witchcraft. What had the druid Saman called her? Upir. Life-stealer.

Kim embraced what she was becoming. She strode both sides of the life-death boundary, one foot in this world and one in the land of the dead.

And she'd never felt so alive.

—⁓—

Standing beside Carol on the invisible platform she'd created, Arn watched as she shifted her attention to the spot where Alan and his Forsworn carved their way through the leading edge of the new arrivals to this battle. Then she did something he had never seen her do before: modify the shield that blocked magic from raining down on the Forsworn so that it reflected and magnified the image of the Chosen. The projection made the scene visible to the tens of thousands who struggled on the battleground.

His image ten times larger than life, the soldiers watched the Chosen hurl himself into the fray, a whirling menace that split asunder all who faced him, hacking limbs, heads, and torsos with devastating force.

Arn felt Carol's mind touch his, just as he had foreseen that she would be forced to do. All the mystic power she wielded was draining her. Unless Arn could find her a path to victory, her strength would eventually fail. And when Carol died, so would Arn and everyone who fought alongside them.

Yet the further he explored his visions, the less distinct they became, eventually disappearing in a fog of possibilities it was beyond his skill to penetrate. Now would be a good time for Landrel to put in one of his mysterious appearances, but that just wasn't happening.

Arn sucked in a deep breath and contemplated what he was about to do. If this failed, he would usher in the events he was trying so hard to prevent. He looked at Carol. She stood proud, her white eyes staring out over the battlefield while she used her dog's vision to see. The wind whipped her dark-brown hair around her shoulders as she spread her hands to fend off another round of attacks by the most powerful of the enemy priests.

Where was Kragan? Why had he not taken this opportunity to enter the fight? These were the questions he knew Carol was asking herself. Sensing his intent, Carol released her link to Zaislus and firmly linked her mind to Arn's.

Shoving aside his worries, Arn braced himself, then emptied the contents of his small pouch into his right hand, embracing the artifact that swept them from reality and into the myriad futures that spun out before them.

23

Paradiis
YOR 415, Early Winter

Cloaked in invisibility atop the city wall, Kragan looked out across the battleground where tens of thousands now fought and died. He magnified the scene. Carol Rafel and Blade floated high above the battlefield, bathed in fire and lightning by hundreds of Dieve's priests and acolytes. A short distance to the east of her, the Chosen fought like a madman, striking such terror into the souls of his foes that they shrank back before him and the hundreds of his bald followers.

The blind witch whom he had sought through the centuries created an air lens that reflected this vision for all to see. And the dread the sight produced within the armies of Jogi, Paradiis, and Vurtsid was palpable. This view of the Chosen also stiffened the spines of the thousands of beleaguered clansmen, resurrecting the hope that the arrival of King Troc's army had destroyed.

Kragan felt the three fingers that dangled from his necklace, tempted to throw his own might against the young woman whom Landrel had predicted might be his downfall. But no. He would comply with the prophecy and gather the last three of the mystic shards that Landrel's offspring had secured within the temples of Sadamad.

With all eyes locked on the earthshaking fight beyond these walls, Kragan knew it was time. He hefted the pack containing the cloth-wrapped scrying globe that he used to contact Svaty up higher on his shoulder. Then he stepped off the city side of the wall and floated to the street below. Having learned a valuable lesson about the dangers of flying while confronting powerful adversaries, he walked through the streets toward the central plaza.

Beneath the stormy skies, the roads were empty of civilian traffic. And with the vast majority of Paradiis's soldiers fighting outside the city or arrayed atop the battlements, he had the streets mostly to himself.

Even the park that surrounded the turquoise temple lay vacant. Like the army, the city's priests had been deployed to support the battle. Kragan knew that only the sacred triumvirate remained inside the temple to guard the precious artifact within the altar's cornerstone.

When he climbed the steps to the inlaid temple doors, he found them locked. Kragan was not surprised. He summoned an earth elemental he favored. Willing Dalg to give several of the stones in the wall the consistency of smoke, he created a portal just large enough for him to walk through. Clutching the three fingers of amplification in his left hand, he called forth elementals from the planes of air, fire, and water to shield him in webs of magic. Then Kragan stepped through the wall.

The three priestesses of the triumvirate lashed out at him in a coordinated attack as he emerged. The foremost of the clerics sent forth bolts of light that Kragan quenched with darkness. Another attempted to encase him in ice, while the third slashed an air-blade into the space occupied by the wielder.

Kragan deflected the ethereal sword, using it to shatter the ice as it formed. The triumvirate repeatedly struck at him as he stood before them, their growing desperation showing in the lines of concentration on their faces. A slow grin spread across Kragan's face. Only one person in the world had the potential to challenge him, and at this moment she was occupied.

He extended his right hand, pulling writhing tendrils of darkness from the turquoise ceiling. Seeing their danger, the triumvirate shielded themselves inside gleaming domes of light. The smoky strands attacked their defenses, sprouting tentacles that crawled across each barrier, seeking entry. Several of the dark worms burrowed into the protective brightness only to be forced backward as the priestesses reinforced the cracks in their armor.

Obsidian strands crawled from the marble floor beneath the feet of the nearest of Kragan's opponents, worming their way beneath her robes. The woman's eyes widened in shock as the vessels in her neck bulged and blackened. With her shrieks echoing from the walls, the priestess's brilliant dome collapsed. The rest of the shadow filaments wriggled into her eyes, nose, and mouth.

The woman fell to the floor, her body convulsing as she clawed globs of flesh from her own face. Kragan concentrated on keeping the priestess alive, letting the spectacle continue for the benefit of the other two clergywomen. Then he turned his attention to the rightmost of the surviving wielders, savoring the horror in the woman's eyes.

The wielder bathed Kragan in a fountain of flame that scorched the lovely tile wall. Her companion floated several feet above the floor, encasing herself in a globe so bright it hurt Kragan's eyes. The priestess put all her power into strengthening her defenses.

Kragan sneered as he recognized the fire elemental that his current target controlled. His mind snared Krosnele, ripping the being from the priestess's control. It turned on its former master with a heat so intense that it seared the floor beneath the dying Paradiisian torch.

He turned his attention to the hovering lone survivor. Kragan raised his hand, palm outward toward the shining orb within which his foe sheltered. Wisps of the sphere's glowing essence drifted to Kragan's cupped fingers to form a ball that was a miniature replica of the larger globe.

Ever so slowly, Kragan closed his fingers around it, squeezing against the resistance he felt there. He continued to tighten his grip and, ever so slowly, the orb within his hand contracted. And as that ball grew smaller, so did its larger twin. The pressure against Kragan's clutch increased to the point that it momentarily stopped contracting.

Light leaked between Kragan's fingers as he brought more power to bear. In a last desperate act, his opponent dropped her shielding and sent a dozen glittering bolts at Kragan, forcing him to briefly shift from the attack to block the arcane lances, halting them in midair a hand-span from his face. With his will amplified by the artifacts that dangled from his necklace, Kragan snatched control of the elemental being the woman wielded, forging the magical lances into a glittering blade that streaked into his enemy and exploded.

The light in the room dimmed so suddenly that it left Kragan blinking. As his eyes adjusted, he saw that the white altar was splattered with red. Only a few of the candles atop it remained aglow. Pieces of the corpse lay scattered beneath the spot where the wielder had floated.

Kragan lowered his hand, marveling at what Queen Severak's paranoia had wrought. Unwilling to place her faith in any outsider, the merchant queen of Paradiis had trusted only her three most powerful wielders to guard this altar. She'd told Jogi's queen to send Svaty, the mightiest of Dieve's disciples, and the rest of Jogi's priesthood out to confront the Chosen and his blind witch. At Kragan's urging, Afacere had agreed to this strategy.

Kragan walked to the altar and knelt to examine the cornerstone, setting his pack on the marble floor. Kragan would need to place the time stone against its counterparts from Jogi and Vurtsid. These rested within Queen Severak's royal vault.

Using Dalg to dissolve the mortar that held the cornerstone in place, Kragan slid the precious object out of the altar and placed it in his pack. Standing, he cloaked himself in invisibility and walked out through the portal he'd created. He paused in the park to listen to the thunder that confirmed the distant battle yet raged.

A pleasant warmth spread through his chest.

Once Kragan forced his way into Severak's vault, the outcome of this war would no longer matter. That combat was a distraction that had now served its purpose.

24

Southeast of Paradiis
YOR 415, Early Winter

The exhaustion of the fight was a weight on Carol's shoulders. And the artifact that spun Arn and her into a maelstrom of near futures almost dragged her to her knees. Arn's voice in her head helped steady her.

"Don't fight it. Let me be the guide."

"Can you handle this without Landrel's help?"

"We're about to find out."

Carol watched herself and Arn die as her husband stepped through hundreds of realities, knowing that no time at all had passed in the real world. One of his visions dawned with spectacular clarity, revealing the next action she needed to take. Arn released her back into the present, and Carol shifted her attention away from the army that had attacked them from behind. Instead she concentrated on carving a pathway to Paradiis.

A glance through Arn's eyes told her that Alan and his Forsworn had merged forces with the clans. Maintaining her connection to Arn, she added a mental link to her brother.

"Alan. We must get to the city."

"But the walls . . ."

"Let me worry about that. Just get us there."

With part of her mind controlling the dozens of elementals that shielded the clans, the Forsworn, and herself from the ongoing attacks of the priesthood, she lowered herself, Arn, and Zaislus to the ground.

Surrounded by the elite clan warriors who guarded her, she moved out, keeping pace with the renewed attack into the heart of the Paradiis defenders with Arn and Zaislus at her side.

The attacks from the wielders who sought to thwart her intensified such that she needed to weaken her link to Arn, lest his waking dreams prove too great a distraction. She sent Arn a fresh mental request.

"You're overwhelming me. Filter out the bad visions."

Carol decreased her connection to Arn until she could barely feel him, lessening the strain upon her mental resources. But Arn's new filtering had a downside. His mental focus produced such vivid imagery that it threatened to distract Carol from her wielding.

The latest of these visions burned itself into her mind, and she redirected the air elemental Lwellen, forcing the being to deflect myriad bolts targeted at her into the seething mass of Paradiisian troops. A ragged rumble shook the earth beneath Carol's feet as thunder buffeted her.

Alan seized his opportunity and charged through the mass of charred bodies into the stunned soldiers who fought to block his path forward. Less than a hundred paces now separated the Chosen from the city walls. The commanders atop those ramparts ordered their archers to fire indiscriminately into the churning battle below, dropping more of their fellow soldiers than of the Forsworn.

Carol heard Alan's bellow as he burst through the last line of defenders. He raced straight toward the impregnable barrier, his faith in his sister's ability to get him through it absolute. To their credit, none of the two hundred Forsworn hesitated to follow him, but the clan warriors pulled up short of arrow range and turned to block the enemies who pursued them.

Carol halted, pushed her hands out toward Alan and his followers, and lifted them into the air. The Forsworn cascaded onto the battlements like water sprayed from a pipe. Some failed to find purchase or were pushed back over the parapets, yet most survived the initial assault.

Then Arn drowned Carol in another of his dreams.

—⁓—

Alan landed on top of the wall and rolled to his feet, knocking over a handful of archers and sweeping aside two of their fellows with the first stroke of his ax. He dodged to his left to avoid striking Quincy, who tumbled onto the rampart behind him. Kim landed on her feet beside Galad.

To Alan's left a javelin tore open Tudor's throat, but the wound immediately disappeared to open the throat of the man who'd hurled it. An enemy wielder raised her hands to the heavens only to be swallowed by Galad's time-mists before she could complete the spell.

The defenders struggled to react to the stunning turn of events, but Alan discouraged them. Having watched hundreds of his Forsworn die on this day and a score more fail to find their footing atop the wall and plunge to their deaths, he seethed with fury.

Kragan was behind this, and before this was over, Alan would hang the wielder's overlarge head from this parapet. Alongside Quincy, Kat, and Tudor, he butchered his way through the archers and into the soldiers who manned the top of this wall. His forearms, swollen with the blood that fed his muscles, burst free of their gauntlets.

It felt so good to be rid of the constraining armor. He was tempted to shed his chain-and-leather jerkin. Instead he tossed aside his shield to wield Ty's ax with both hands.

As he hurled defenders from the wall, the Chosen's defiant yell echoed through the city.

"Forsworn. To the gates."

—⟋⟋—

Carol experienced what the elite wielder was about to attempt and countered it, feeling the fury in this woman's mind as her wall of fire descended inside the city instead of atop the wall where the Forsworn fought. Carol's mind touched that of the one who thought of herself as High Priestess Svaty.

Their wills clashed, and in her exhausted state, Carol almost faltered. Instead she dropped her partial links to Arn and Alan to direct all her effort at this worthy opponent. Carol reached deep into the woman's memories, seeking those with the most emotional attachment. Better yet, she searched for those this wielder had buried beneath layers of scar tissue.

At first she found nothing of emotional significance. Then all at once she penetrated a protective barrier that blossomed pain.

—⟋⟋—

Svaty held her little girl against her bosom, her tears raining down on her daughter's face. Over and over she sobbed her child's name. Detska. She shifted her eyes to the man whose body lay sprawled across the floor of their kitchen, blood leaking from his eyes, mouth, nose, and ears.

Svaty had done this. She just wished she had killed her drunken husband more slowly, more painfully. She'd put up with his abuse for years, but never had she imagined that he would project his anger on their lovely child, slapping their daughter so hard that his blow snapped her neck. And in doing so, Pijan had unleashed Svaty's magic.

If she could undo this, Svaty would happily forsake the destiny that had called her forth. Instead she buried her daughter, then turned and consumed their house in an inferno that failed to burn away her agony. She had instead buried the trauma so deep in her subconscious that she could never experience its pain again.

Until now.

—⁓—

Carol pried the recollection from its mind-crypt, releasing it into Svaty's consciousness, hating herself for doing so. By the deep, what had she become that she could destroy this woman who merely wanted to defend her goddess and her society? Kragan deserved this, not Svaty. She disentangled her mind from that of the high priestess, leaving Svaty a broken shell.

Outside the walls of Paradiis, Carol straightened and looked at Arn through Zaislus's eyes.

"Find Kragan."

She watched as Arn's eyes acquired the faraway look of his time-sight.

"Done."

—⁓—

Arn didn't know where Kragan was. He knew where he was going to be. The only question was: Could he and Carol get there in time to stop the wielder from becoming unstoppable?

He exited that vision to search for the nearer-term future that would get them into the palace where the royal vault of Paradiis rested. From there he backed off until he was once again in combat mode, sensing what Carol and he needed to do next while maintaining his ability to act in the here and now.

"Take us over that wall."

Carol worked her magic, cloaking herself, Arn, and her dog in invisibility. He knew that she couldn't make them truly invisible. She merely used a variation of the magic that allowed her to lens the air so that it bent light around their little group. If people got within a half dozen paces, they would notice the distortion. Anyone who got closer than that would see them.

Carol levitated them over the high wall, setting them down in a side street beyond the broad avenue where combat raged. He sensed her increase the strength of her mental bond with him.

Arn squeezed the mummified finger in his left hand, sampling hundreds of courses of action in an instant. When he turned into a narrow alley that led northwest, Carol and Zaislus followed.

25

Kragan entered the royal palace through the twenty-foot-high front doors. He walked past the dozen soldiers who guarded the entryway, but halfway across the hall that led to the throne room, he stopped and turned back toward them. Kragan swung his right hand in a wide arc, as if he were tossing coins to the poor.

Instead of coins, twelve glittering razors of solidified air shot from his palm. A dozen heads rolled across the blood-spattered marble floor as the bodies collapsed around them. He whirled as the four soldiers outside the throne room doors began to raise their crossbows, sending more of the deadly scythes their way.

The attack was over in a moment. No alarm sounded. Kragan sent forth a gust of wind that sent the doors crashing open and walked through the growing pool of blood into the presence of stunned royalty. Queen Severak sat on the central throne with King Troc on her left and Queen Afacere on her right. Severak's shrill voice echoed through the chamber.

"Guards, to me."

When nothing happened, she repeated her call.

"I'm afraid your royal guards are indisposed," Kragan said, leaving a trail of bloody footprints as he walked up to the rulers.

He came to a stop three paces in front of Queen Severak.

"Kragan," Afacere said, "what have you done?"

"The question should be: What am I doing? I am here for the key that Queen Severak wears around her skinny royal neck."

"I'll see you burned alive for this," King Troc said.

"You have it backwards."

A flame danced in the air above Kragan's fingers. He flicked it forward, and the king's garments engulfed Troc in a fire so intense that its heat sent the two queens scrambling from their thrones. Before they could flee the room, Kragan bound them in glowing bands of red that suspended them a foot above the floor. Thus were they forced to watch the spectacle until Troc stopped wailing and lay still.

All that remained of the king of Vurtsid was a charred husk and the stench of burned flesh.

Kragan turned and walked up to the two queens, his gaze locked on Severak.

"Since Queen Afacere and I arrived in Paradiis, I have tolerated your derisive looks, all in anticipation of this day."

The sharp-featured queen spat at him, but it halted a foot in front of him, reversed course, and splattered on Severak's face. He summoned the water elemental Boaa, forming a bubble of the liquid around the insolent queen's head. It was longer than he'd expected before Severak became unable to hold her breath and inhaled the fatal lungful of water. Although her panicked convulsions did not take nearly that long, Kragan found them extremely satisfying.

When Severak finally stopped kicking, he released her magical bonds, dropping her corpse to the floor in front of him.

Kragan shifted his attention to Queen Afacere. She looked resplendent in her azure gown, despite the terror that widened her eyes. She floated a foot above the marble floor. The magical cord that bound her arms and legs glowed an angry red as she struggled in vain to free herself. He strode forward, then levitated himself so that he could look directly into her face. When he reached out to gently stroke her cheek, she didn't flinch from his touch. It was one of the traits he admired in this lovely woman.

"Lord Kragan," Queen Afacere said, "I have treated you with great respect and friendship. Surely that means something."

"Indeed. I thank you for that. In return, you shall not suffer the deaths of these other two fools."

The relief on Afacere's face was poignant. Kragan let it linger there for a moment, then snapped her neck.

"Unfortunately, I cannot have a queen who has observed these acts lingering at my back."

Kragan dropped her body beside that of the other queen. Then he knelt beside Severak and unbuttoned her blouse at the neck. He reached inside the garment to extract the key she always wore there, snapping the gold necklace that held it.

He stood and walked away from the three corpses, past the thrones, to the single door in the rear wall of the throne room. Kragan pulled it open, summoned a globe of light, and descended the stone steps of the spiral staircase. Two dozen steps later, he emerged into a short hallway that had been carved through solid granite, coming to a stop before a heavy steel door.

Although he could easily have bypassed the barrier with his earth magic, it was so much more satisfying to slide the iron key into the lock, twist it, and hear the clank of the tumblers dropping into place.

He pushed the heavy door open and stepped into a room too large for the dim globe to illuminate. Kragan increased the light's intensity. The Paradiisian treasure vault was arranged like a small bazaar, with aisles stacked high with items formed of gold, silver, and precious jewels. Apparently the business of being a merchant queen was a profitable one. Kragan had no interest.

He made his way up one row and down another. Then he saw them, two white time stones set atop an ivory pedestal. His heart raced, and his breath came so rapidly it left Kragan slightly dizzy. Stepping up beside the stand, he let his pack slide from his left shoulder, set the bag on the floor, and removed the third time stone, setting it beside the others.

With reverence he slid the stones together so that each touched the other two and stepped back.

At first nothing happened.

Then the stones darkened where all three came together. With agonizing slowness, the darkness spread through the bricks as all three acquired the consistency of fog. The mists flowed off the pedestal in rivers that Kragan dared not touch.

As if a breeze had entered the vault, the haze cleared. There, on the ivory surface, sat three more of the skeletal fingers. Whereas what hung from Kragan's necklace consisted of two thumbs and an index finger, these shards consisted of a thumb and two index digits.

Kragan grasped the Landrel shards that dangled from his necklace in his left fist. Then, with a trembling right hand, he reached for the other three.

—ɷ—

Kim moved forward in the Forsworn formation, positioning herself just far enough behind Alan to avoid most of the crimson that sprayed from his whirling ax. Tudor and Quincy pressed their way forward through the Paradiisian defenders on Alan's left while Kat fought to his right.

Galad once again swathed the tightly bunched Forsworn in his rychly mists. Without Carol's shielding they needed protection from the enemy wielders who attempted to rain destruction on those who breached the Paradiisian defenders atop the city wall. Just as importantly, Alan needed to take the main gates before these same magic wielders could shift their attention to the clansmen who were pinned against the outer wall by the army that had been the late arrival on that battlefield.

Alan fought so close to the leading edge of the mist that he could see no more than two paces in front of him. But that enabled him and his forward companions to deal with any wielders, archers, or spearmen from close range as they emerged into the zone of accelerated time.

Suddenly the time-mist rolled over the hundreds of soldiers who were bunched in defense of the gate, warriors jammed so tightly against the barrier that even Alan was having difficulty pushing through them. Everywhere Kim looked, bladed weapons bristled.

Dozens more of the Forsworn threw themselves at the defenders. Then the rest joined the fray. Kim almost lost herself to the dizziness that threatened her consciousness as she struggled to simultaneously heal her people and kill their enemies. As was the case throughout the fight, she failed to save most of those who fell, impaled on shaft or blade. But she saved Alan and those who protected his flanks.

Amid the desperate slaughter, Kim was shocked to see Alan heave from its moorings the tree-trunk-thick crossbar that held the gates shut. When he tossed the log aside, the gates swung inward under the pressure of the clansmen outside the city walls.

While Galad funneled his time-mists outward to envelop their allies, the Forsworn parted to allow the clans to pour into Paradiis.

—⚏—

Carol reached the closed palace doors with Arn and Zaislus on either side. The urgency she felt in Arn's cascading visions pulled her forward. When she pushed on the rightmost door, it didn't move. Neither did the other door budge. When she knocked and got no response, Carol burst the doors from their hinges.

The pools of blood and beheaded guards told her all she needed to know. Kragan had beaten them here.

Carol broke into a run that Arn and Zaislus matched. The sight of the three dead bodies in the throne room didn't slow her. Arn's visions were reduced to a handful that fought for dominance. All of them led to the open door on the far wall.

As she raced down the spiral staircase, three more of Arn's possible futures faded away. By the time she reached the doorway into the vault, only two possible outcomes remained.

Carol walked past several rows of stacked treasure just in time to see Kragan grasp something atop a white pedestal. The small man spun to face her, a smile on his face. With one hand clasping his necklace and the other gripping something else, he stepped forward.

"Welcome, Carol. Unfortunately, you've arrived just a moment too late."

As magic curled from the wielder's fists, Carol summoned as much elemental protection as she could, wrapped her shielding around her small group, and braced herself for the inevitable.

When the vortex struck her, she cried out in despair. She hadn't fallen, but she knew with certainty that she would. She would die and so would her one true love. And as her defenses started to fray, Arn stepped forward, his left hand clenched so tightly that the veins seemed to pop from the skin of his forearm.

"Link us to Kragan. Now."

A vision of chaos formed in her mind, but she did as Arn demanded. And as Carol did so, she, Arn, and Kragan became one.

—◁◿▷—

In the midst of Kragan's casting, everything changed. The world blurred around him as a dizzying progression of visions filled his mind. He found himself propelled through thousands of scenarios that were so vivid he could not distinguish them from reality.

They could not all be true.

Despite gripping all six of the ancient artifacts, he was too distracted to gain control. He died hundreds of times in many ways. He killed Carol. He killed Blade. His own magic consumed him.

Kragan lost himself in the kaleidoscope of images, wandering through realities that could not be. He could not find his way out of the madness that held him in its clutches. One thought crystallized in his reeling consciousness: if he didn't free himself from this maelstrom of hallucinations, his mind would break.

He pounded his temple with his right fist. He screamed. He wailed. Still the visions kept coming.

Then, just as he reached the limit of his strength to fight off the encroaching insanity, a figure stepped from the shadows. Recognition burned its way into Kragan's seething brain.

Landrel.

The dead Endarian said nothing but motioned for Kragan to follow him. And despite the knowledge that this was just another manifestation of his madness, Kragan complied.

—⁓—

As familiar as Carol had become with accompanying Arn into his waking dreams, the vision storm shook her. He was using all his amplified ability to peer farther and farther into the possible futures that branched out before them.

Kragan staggered through the hallucinations, desperately searching for something stabilizing to cling to. But there was no firm footing here. Everything changed as one reality after another swept by them.

When Kragan wandered through the hazy boundaries between dreamscapes, Carol lost sight of him but followed Arn to regain sight of the distraught wielder. She watched Kragan pound his head with his fist, heard him howl his misery at the universe. And as she observed the breaking of this evil man's mind, Carol's hopes for victory coalesced.

Suddenly an unknown Endarian stepped into the future that she, Arn, and Kragan occupied. He gestured at Kragan, and the wielder followed the man into another vision. Carol rushed to follow, but when she stepped through the boundary, she found only Arn.

"Where is he?" she asked.

"With Landrel."

"Where?"

"I lost them."

A terrible realization dawned upon her.

"Take us out of here."

She felt Arn shift his concentration, ever so gradually guiding them out of the distant futures along paths that brought them ever closer to the present. When she again felt real stone beneath her feet, Carol found herself standing in total darkness.

She summoned a light, and through Arn's eyes, she saw that they stood beside Zaislus in the treasure chamber. Looking around, she felt her stomach clench.

Kragan was gone. And so were Landrel's artifacts.

—◦∭◦—

Kragan opened his eyes to find himself lying in an alley on the west side of the palace. He sat up, opened his right hand, and breathed out a huge sigh of relief. The three shards of Landrel's Trident were still in his palm. And the other three still dangled from his necklace.

He was so drained, he could barely manage the spell that lensed the air around him, providing him with invisibility from all those who were more than three paces away. Thick smoke hung over Paradiis. When he looked to the southeast, he saw why. Flames rose into the sky over a large section of the city.

Kragan turned and headed west as fast as his legs could carry him, hoping that all he needed was a few minutes to clear his head and recover from the nausea that plagued him. The fact that no one was in the streets aided his progress. He understood why. Any soldiers would have rushed to the site of the breach that had allowed the army of the Chosen to enter the city.

Apparently the son of High Lord Rafel was intent on burning Paradiis to the ground. Kragan didn't intend to be anywhere nearby when that happened.

When he reached the harbor, he saw what he had come for. Sailors scurried across the upper deck of King Troc's royal galley, waiting only for their monarch's arrival to set sail.

He inhaled deeply, feeling the air fill his lungs, making his head feel better. Clutching all six of the skeletal fingers, he strode to the gangplank, uncloaking himself and hurling the guards at its base into the sea. As he walked up onto the deck, a dozen sailors fired crossbows at him. The bolts came to a stop, quivering as if they had imbedded themselves in oak ten feet from him.

Flames flowed from Kragan's fists, turning the men into human torches and launching them into the bay.

He stopped and addressed the rest of the shocked sailors, amplifying his voice for all to hear.

"Do you all want to die like those fools, or are you willing to set sail under my command?"

The ship's captain stepped out onto the deck.

"Get off my ship or I will put you off in pieces."

"Wrong answer."

Kragan sent five air scythes streaking at the captain, severing his legs, arms, and head from his body. The wielder swung his gaze across the sailors and officers who stared down at him from the upper deck and rigging.

"Decide."

An officer Kragan took to be the second in command stepped forward. "We will set sail."

"Then cast off. I want to be out of this bay before the sun sinks below the horizon."

The officer yelled orders that sent the sailors scurrying to their tasks. When they shoved off and sailed westward out of the bay, Kragan stood at the prow, feeling the cold sea breeze ruffle his hair. The continent of Sadamad had nothing left to offer him.

But Endar did.

26

Paradiis
YOR 415, Early Winter

Carol walked out of the royal palace with Arn and Zaislus at her side. It wasn't all the bodies that sickened her. It was the knowledge that they had been so close to breaking Kragan's mind only to have Landrel save him. Kragan had escaped with six of the nine fragments of Landrel's Trident.

The sinking sun painted the billowing clouds of smoke that rose above the southeastern side of Paradiis bloodred. With Kragan gone, she needed to get to where combat yet raged.

"To the wall?" Arn asked.

"Yes."

Carol considered flying them to the battlements, but she was so wrung out she needed to conserve what mystic energy she retained for whatever she would find there. Besides, she couldn't maintain such a wielding while passing through the time-mists that Galad would have summoned. They jogged through the streets, guided along the paths less traveled by Arn's time-sight. Having put away the token of the ancient wielder of time magic, he returned his focus to the futures that lay right before them.

When Arn came to a sudden halt, Carol pulled up beside him.

"What is it?" she asked.

"The clans have entered the city. They and the Forsworn hold the main gate and the city wall," he replied.

"What of the enemy wielders?"

"Galad's mists have blocked their attacks."

"Take me to Alan."

When they emerged from a narrow alley onto the broad avenue that led to the gates, they saw the time-mists that swathed the city wall and battlements. As they made their way through that boundary, the zone they'd just left fogged over and the way ahead cleared.

Perhaps a hundred of the bald Forsworn manned the wall above the gate, and Carol could see thousands of clansmen at the battlements for as far as she could see in either direction. Alan saw them and descended from the wall to meet them. He was so covered in drying blood that only his thick body allowed Carol to recognize him.

"The attack has stopped?" she asked.

"For the moment. We've repelled three assaults, each weaker than the preceding. Five thousand clansmen guard the battlements. Vahltehr has sent another two thousand warriors through the city to root out any pockets of resistance within. What of Kragan?"

Carol didn't try to keep the bitterness from her voice.

"Arn and I had him at our mercy. Landrel helped Kragan escape with all six of the Sadamad artifacts."

"How is that possible?"

"I don't know."

"But Landrel created his scroll to help us defeat Kragan."

"So we thought."

"Kragan murdered Landrel. Why would the Endarian aid his escape? What game is Landrel playing?"

"One that we don't understand." Carol forced her frustration from her thoughts. "What can I do to help here?"

Alan pointed back toward the city that lay hidden beyond the time-mist boundary. "Can you do something about the fire that rages out there?"

"That I can."

Carol turned and led the way back through the mists and into the city. She turned her attention to the blaze spreading through several houses, barracks, and shops. Fingers of flame reached into the sky.

She lifted her arms, pulling clouds over the city. The downpour stretched across the whole city and over the countryside where the enemy armies remained. The chill torrent that drenched her and Arn couldn't match the ice in her soul.

—⁂—

The night passed without another attack on the wall that protected Paradiis. Arn stood atop the battlements beside Carol as Galad dispelled his time-mists. Now, with the arrival of dawn, it was time to see what lay beyond the fog.

What he saw didn't surprise Arn. His time-sight had told him what the fading wisps were most likely to reveal. Corpses lay strewn across the battlefield as flocks of carrion birds circled in the sky, their black wings lit by the rising sun. The chill in the morning air turned Arn's breath into visible puffs.

Long columns of soldiers wound away from Paradiis to the southeast. The army that had conducted the surprise attack into the rear of the Chosen's was that of Vurtsid. With no word from their king and with the clans in control of Paradiis, their leaders had apparently decided to abandon the field and return to their homeland.

The few thousand soldiers who remained in camps beyond these fortifications wore the uniforms of Paradiis and Jogi. A contingent approached the gates under a flag of truce. Alan and Vahltehr, accompanied by the hundred surviving Forsworn, strode out through the gates to meet them.

Arn spotted Kim among the group of Forsworn closest to Alan, her long auburn hair and brown skin standing out among all the pale, shorn warriors. The sight of her triggered a series of disturbing visions that Arn thrust from his head. The Endarian princess that he, John, and Ty had rescued from vorg slavers was like a sister to him. He refused to allow himself to suffer any dark foretellings where Kim was concerned.

"Are they surrendering?" Carol asked.

"Both the Paradiisian soldiers and the Jogi troops have their families within these walls," Arn said. "They just want to end this."

"The clans won't want to remain in the city for long," Carol said. "They will forge new treaties with Jogi and Paradiis, extracting whatever tribute they desire. Then the clansmen will return to their homes in the Kalnai Mountains as victors, bearing their spoils of war."

"But we will continue our mission," Arn said, his disappointment deepening his voice. "We will find Kragan and kill him, or he will kill us. Either way, our task will be done."

—⟋⟍—

For the first time in recent memory, Alan enjoyed the luxury of a hot bath. It took two tubs of water to rid him of the dried blood that caked his body. Kat scrubbed him clean with a stiff brush and rinsed him with a fresh bucket of water before he stepped into the second bath. There she joined him. They didn't make love, merely luxuriating in the hot water while her back pressed against his chest. But as he relaxed with Kat in his arms, he couldn't purge the image of Kimber from his head.

After he climbed from the tub to towel off, he watched Katrin do the same, savoring the urges her lean body stoked inside him. Unfortunately, the meeting for which he now dressed produced an even more urgent call.

He strode into the Paradiisian throne room, accompanied by Kat, Tudor, and Quincy, their footsteps echoing through the vast space. Servants had removed the bodies of Queen Afacere, King Troc, and Queen Severak, but the charring and bloodstains still marred the floor. The smell of death wafted to his nose, so familiar to him that he paid it no heed.

Carol, Arn, Kim, and Galad sat alongside the two surviving Kalnai chieftains, Vahltehr and Horsky, along one side of a long table. Arrayed opposite them sat representatives of the governments of Jogi, Vurtsid, and Paradiis. Next to Carol, an empty chair waited for Alan. He motioned for his companions to stop and took his seat.

Carol was the first to speak.

"Lord Alan, let me introduce the representatives with whom we will negotiate the terms of the peace that will follow these weeks of struggle."

Alan noted the formal phrasing his sister used but didn't interrupt her.

"On the left is Mudry. She is high councillor to the former queen of Paradiis and acting ruler of this city."

The lean woman who wore a brown robe with a chin-high collar nodded ever so slightly, her tightly pressed lips forming a straight line across her face.

"The man in the center," Carol said, "is Recnik, the senior senator representing Jogi."

The senator's snow-white hair framed a puffy, olive face. The man made no move to acknowledge Alan's presence.

"And lastly," Carol said, "representing Vurtsid, is King Troc's adviser, Poradcu."

The graceful woman wore a low-cut chartreuse gown. But her smile as she met his gaze surprised him.

"I take it that you are the one the clansmen call the Chosen."

"Yes."

The smile melted from her face. "You defeated the army of Rukkumine only to invade our lands and conquer the combined forces of Jogi, Paradiis, and Vurtsid. What terms of surrender would you force upon our people?"

Vahltehr leaned forward, pounding his fist on the table.

"Do not dare act as though you are the aggrieved parties. Your sister city of Rukkumine invaded our mountains and attacked my son and the Chosen. After we defeated Rukkumine, Queen Afacere sent Jogi's army against us. When we pursued her broken horde into the north, Paradiis and Vurtsid joined forces with Afacere to destroy us. By the deep, we will set the terms for the reparations you owe us."

Alan leaned forward, resting his elbows on the table.

"Chief Vahltehr speaks the truth. But there is an underlying factor of which all of you are probably unaware."

"What would that be?" Mudry asked, disbelief obvious in both voice and manner.

"I and my followers pursued a powerful wielder of dark sorcery, a small man who ingratiated himself to Queen Afacere. We have evidence that his council convinced Afacere to attack the clans. After her army's defeat, this wielder orchestrated the queen's plan to recruit King Troc and Queen Severak to help destroy us."

Recnik's white eyebrows rose, furrowing the Jogi man's forehead.

"What is the name of this wielder you seek?"

"Kragan."

Recnik's fury pulled a ruddiness into his face and narrowed his eyes to slits.

"Spawn of the deepest pits, Afacere's councillors and I tried to convince her not to listen to that conjurer. Even General Prikazca failed to bring Afacere to her senses. Kragan entranced our queen and led us to this disaster." Recnik slumped back in his chair. "Now Kragan is gone. Where he has gone, we do not know."

"And," Carol said, "Kragan was the one who stole the precious Landrel artifacts from each of your cities. We also believe his thefts started the war between Rukkumine and Varjupaik."

Angry muttering commenced among the three city-state representatives. Alan saw Clan Chief Horsky start to interrupt but held up a hand that stopped him. It was best to allow these people some time to come to terms with what they had just heard. Then, with a nod, Alan signaled for Horsky to continue.

"So you see," Horsky said, "this Kragan fellow has used you to prevent us from recovering the stolen artifacts and returning them to the temples to which Landrel's children gifted them. We have all paid for the wielder's wrongdoing with the lives of thousands of our warriors."

The brown-robed representative of Paradiis fixed her eyes on Alan.

"Chosen. What would you have of us in compensation? Will you install clansmen to rule our cities?"

"The clan chiefs and I have discussed this. They have no desire to rule Paradiis, nor Jogi, nor Vurtsid. Chief Vahltehr and Chief Horsky will set the amount of tribute that you must pay for the families of the fallen. You will also be required to sign new treaties guaranteeing clan rights to the entire Kalnai Mountain Range."

"What else?" asked Recnik.

"Then the clansmen will return to their mountain homes."

"And what of you and your followers?" Mudry asked.

"I will require a dozen ships, stocked with supplies to carry a thousand warriors from Sadamad to Endar. Once that is done, I will gather my followers and depart."

"And Kragan?" asked Recnik.

"He has all of the Landrel artifacts that belonged to Sadamad. He will try to take the others from Endar. I intend to stop him."

Another babble of conversation started among the representatives. When it quieted, the sultry Poradcu of Vurtsid spoke for them all.

"We deem your terms fair. Let us begin to get you all gone."

—∿—

Carol stood in the amphitheater where thousands of clansmen had gathered to celebrate their victory and to bid farewell to the Chosen of the Dread Lord. Through the eyes of Zaislus, she scanned the crowd. Of the nearly twenty thousand warriors and druids who had marched from the Kalnai Mountains, fewer than half would return to their highland homes.

Alan's Forsworn had suffered the heaviest casualties. But as happened after each battle the Chosen fought, hundreds of those who had watched him from a distance had sworn the death oath and pledged themselves to his service. These would remain at his side rather than return to their mountain-clan homes.

But standing next to Alan on the dais in the amphitheater's center were the closest of his shorn companions: Katrin, Quincy, and now Tudor. The sight of that small group of friends, the memories of all they'd endured and accomplished, brought a tightness to Carol's throat.

The ceremonial drinking and dancing continued until well past midnight, but she and Arn departed long before the party ended. She illuminated the room they had chosen within the royal palace. It was spacious, with a comfortable bed, an attached washroom, and a balcony, the sort of accommodation that would have been reserved for visiting merchant lords and ladies. After so long traveling and warring, the opulence seemed decadent.

Carol untied her bedroll and spread it upon the floor, but not because she wanted to sleep there. Kneeling, she petted Zaislus as she stared down at the twin dowels that the blanket had wrapped. The *Scroll of Landrel.* Carol had spent so much time studying the document, interpreting the prophecy contained within, that she had come to believe she understood it and its Endarian creator. The sight of the thing now filled her with revulsion.

She picked up the scroll and followed Arn out onto the third-floor balcony. Her big dog stood on his hind legs against the narrow railing to let Carol gaze out over the city. The streets had been washed clean by the rainstorm she had summoned to quench the inferno that had burned a wide swath of the southeastern section of the city.

"How many societies must we destroy?" she asked.

"This is Kragan's doing, not ours. I don't care to experience a world in which he becomes a god."

"But even with your time-sight, amplified by one of the most powerful shards of Landrel's Trident, we failed to stop him. He may be a god already."

"No. Even though he has six of the nine fragments, we almost destroyed him."

"Landrel's ghost betrayed us," she said, holding out the parchment. "Landrel has used this scroll to manipulate us."

"Perhaps we've just failed to understand what he's trying to tell us."

"We saw him guide Kragan to safety. This deep-spawned prophecy is the tool Landrel is using to manipulate us."

Carol slammed the scroll down onto the balcony's stone floor.

The dowels rolled apart just enough to reveal the drawing of Carol, Jaa'dra's image branded into her bare shoulder. The sight of it, through Zaislus's eyes, pulled forth a fury that balled her hands into fists.

"Jaa'dra."

She snared the being in bands of iron will, drawing it from its elemental plane to produce a blaze that consumed the scroll, wooden dowels and all. She released Jaa'dra and turned her back on the pile of ash. But through Zaislus's eyes she shared an image that spun her around and dropped her to her knees beside the smoldering remnants.

"Gods."

She sent forth a weak gust of wind, blowing the ashes away from the slender object that replaced her fury with a sense of wonder.

There on the blackened floor, an undamaged mummified center finger curled directly toward her. Feeling her trepidation, her dog stepped between Carol and the thing that appeared to threaten her, a low growl rumbling in his throat.

Arn's words robbed Carol of what little breath she retained.

"It would seem that Landrel is not yet done with us."

ACKNOWLEDGMENTS

I want to thank my lovely wife, Carol, for her undying support and inspiration during our thirty-eight years of marriage. This project could never have happened without her.

I also want to thank Alan Werner for the many hours he spent in my company storyboarding and brainstorming the bones of this story.

Thanks go out to the hundreds of my beta readers who provided feedback on the early drafts of this novel.

Finally, I want to thank my wonderful editor, Clarence Haynes, for helping me refine yet another story.

ABOUT THE AUTHOR

 Richard Phillips was born in Roswell, New Mexico, in 1956. He graduated from the United States Military Academy at West Point in 1979 and qualified as a US Army Ranger, going on to serve as an officer in the army. He earned a master's degree in physics from the Naval Postgraduate School in 1989, completing his thesis work at Los Alamos National Laboratory. After working as a research associate at Lawrence Livermore National Laboratory, he returned to the army to complete his tour of duty.

Richard is the author of several science fiction and fantasy series, including The Rho Agenda (*The Second Ship*, *Immune*, and *Wormhole*); The Rho Agenda Inception (*Once Dead*, *Dead Wrong*, and *Dead Shift*); The Rho Agenda Assimilation (*The Kasari Nexus*, *The Altreian Enigma*, and *The Meridian Ascent*); and *Mark of Fire*, *Prophecy's Daughter*, *Curse of the Chosen*, and *The Shattered Trident* in the epic Endarian Prophecy series. Richard lives with his wife, Carol, in Phoenix, Arizona. For more information, visit www.rhoagenda.com.